D0016564

HEROES LIKE US

Books by Onjali Q. Raúf

The Boy at the Back of the Class

The Star Outside My Window

The Night Bus Hero

Heroes Like Us

ONJALI Q. RAÚF

DELACORTE PRESS

Dedicated to every child seeking answers to their questions about the way the world treats refugees and the difficult realities of food poverty

 Published in the United States by Delacorte Press, an imprint of Random House Children's Books, a division of Penguin Random House LLC, New York. "The Day We Met the Queen" originally published in paperback by Orion Children's Books, an imprint of Hachette Children's Group, part of Hodder and Stroughton, London, UK, in 2020. "The Great Food Bank Heist" originally published in the United Kingdom by Barrington Stoke, London, in 2021.

Delacorte Press is a registered trademark and the colophon is a trademark of Penguin Random House LLC.

Visit us on the Web! rhcbooks.com

Educators and librarians, for a variety of teaching tools, visit us at RHTeachersLibrarians.com

Library of Congress Cataloging-in-Publication Data
Names: Raúf, Onjali Q, author.
Title: Heroes like us : two stories / Onjali Q Raúf.
Description: First edition. | New York : Delacorte Press, [2022] | Audience: Ages 8–12. | Summary: Two stories featuring ten-year-old Ahmet, the Most Famous Refugee Boy in the World, and his friends, who stood up for Ahmet, and other refugee children like him, in Britain.
Identifiers: LCCN 2021050614 (print) | LCCN 2021050615 (ebook) | ISBN 978-0-593-48819-5 (hardcover) | ISBN 978-0-593-48820-1 (library binding) | ISBN 978-0-593-48821-8 (ebook)
Subjects: CYAC: Refugees—Fiction. | Friendship—Fiction. | Syrians—England—London—Fiction. | London (England)—Fiction. | England—Fiction. | LCGFT: Fiction.
Classification: LCC PZ7.1.R378 He 2022 (print) | LCC PZ7.1.R378 (ebook) | DDC [Fic]—dc23

The text of this book is set in 13-point Warnock Pro Light.
Interior design by Cathy Bobak

Printed in the United States of America
10 9 8 7 6 5 4 3 2 1
First Edition

Contents

THE DAY WE MET THE QUEEN

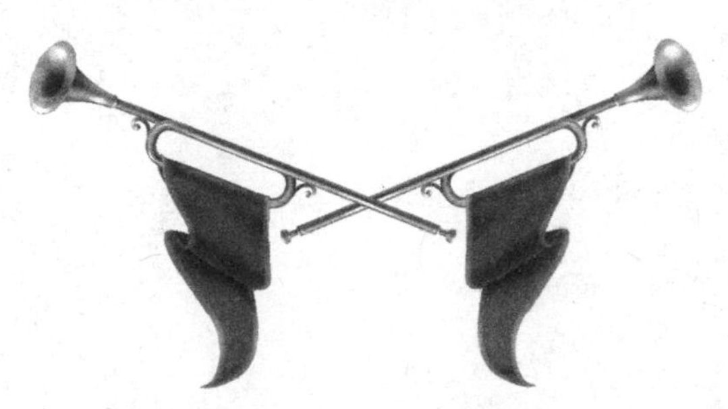

1

A Very Royal Assembly

"Can you believe it? Can you *believe* we're going to see the Queen tomorrow in *actual* real life!"

I looked at Michael. We were standing by the bus stop, waiting for Tom and Josie. Michael pushed his glasses even farther up his nose and, holding the card to the light, stared at it hard—just like shopkeepers do when they think your money isn't real.

But we both knew the invitation *was* real.

The card was so thick it wouldn't let any light through. The writing was fancy and swirly and there was a thick blob of shiny red wax on the envelope. All those things reminded us that the actual real-life Queen of England had sent it and was expecting us to join her for tea tomorrow.

I got my own invitation out from my backpack and held it up to the light too. Not because I wanted to check if it was real but because I wanted to look as important as Michael did. Holding stuff up to the light always makes things seem more serious and scientific than just looking down at them in your hands. I guess that's why people in detective shows on TV are always doing it, even when the room they're in is dark, and holding something up doesn't make a single bit of difference.

"Hey!" called Tom as he hurried toward us. Josie was following him and waving as she dribbled her football. Tom's blond hair was so spiky today it made his head look as if lots of tiny, shiny pyramids had suddenly sprouted up on top of it. Josie's red hair was in a short, thick braid, which looked like a piece of twisted boat rope that someone had cut off in the middle. You knew it was an important day if Josie's hair was in a braid, because she hates her hair being touched or brushed almost as much as she hates beetroot.

"You look . . . different," said Michael, staring at Josie's hair as if he wasn't quite sure what she had done to herself.

Josie shrugged. "It's for the assembly. Mum and Dad promised me tickets to the West Ham game next week if I let them braid it, so I thought I might as well. Even if it does make me look stupid. I mean, look at it!" Grabbing the end of the braid, she pulled it around the back of her neck and over her shoulder to try and make it reach her mouth. But it was too short. "What's the point of it?" she asked, shaking her head. For Josie, hair existed for only one reason—so you could suck on the ends of it when you were nervous or needed help thinking. And to do that, hair needed to be loose and free—and unbrushed.

"Did you bring your invitations?" I asked.

Tom nodded and reached up to check that his hair was still super spiky. "Mine's in my bag. But . . ." Dropping his arms, he scowled and added in a whisper, "Mum framed it!"

Josie snickered. "What? What for?"

"I don't know." Tom shrugged. "She said anything

from anyone royal should always be framed. Especially something from the Queen. She even framed the envelope!"

"Oh . . . ," said Michael, looking down at his frameless invitation as if it was suddenly a disappointment.

"Do you have the list of questions?" asked Tom, looking at me.

I nodded and patted my backpack. Ever since we had known we were going to have tea with the Queen of England, me and Tom and Ahmet and Michael and Josie had spent nearly every break time writing down all the questions we wanted to ask her. In the end, we had fifty-two questions ready, but then our teacher, Mrs. Khan, had said maybe we should cut it down to just two questions each—because the Queen was nearly one hundred years old, and being asked fifty-two questions might make her fall into a coma. Now we were going to read out the questions in morning assembly and show everyone our invitations and explain why we were going to see the Queen. It made my stomach feel funny every time I thought about it.

"Bus is coming!" said Josie, picking up her football and joining the long line of people in front of us. I put my invitation away carefully between two of my workbooks and, quickly zipping up my backpack, jumped on board the bus to school. Running up the stairs, we made our way to the front seats.

"Hope Ahmet remembers to bring his invitation," I said as I squished up next to Tom. "Do you think his foster mum will frame his too? His is probably even more special than ours."

Tom shrugged. "Maybe . . ."

"Anyone else really nervous?" asked Josie, pulling her braid again and trying even harder to make it reach her mouth. "I keep worrying I'll forget everything. I hate assemblies . . ."

Me and Michael and Tom fell quiet, because we were all starting to feel nervous too. None of us had ever been asked to get up in front of the whole entire school and speak at an assembly before.

Usually, assembly was the best part of the day—because you could just sit and pretend to listen even if sometimes you weren't listening at all. Even the teachers like assembly because they don't have to be working or trying to keep everyone under control. You can tell that teachers love assembly more than anything else because they always want to get there early and then when it starts, they sit and smile as if they're thinking about something much more fun than what they're actually listening to.

But today, instead of Mrs. Sanders, our head teacher, staring out at us through her big, square glasses, me and Tom and Josie and Michael and Ahmet were going to be the ones onstage in the huge main hall. All because the Most Famous Woman on the Whole Entire Planet had invited us to her palace for tea.

And that was because of Ahmet, the Most Famous Refugee Boy in the World, who had not only let us be his friends but had made every single one of us almost as famous as he was. Just because we had tried to help him find his family and stop the Queen and the government from closing the gates and borders to refugees like him. I hadn't thought any of those things would make us famous. But for some reason, grown-ups get excited about things that should be normal, and that makes you famous somehow.

"As long as I don't forget what I'm supposed to say and go blank, I don't care what happens," said Tom. "There is *nothing* worse than going blank! One time, back in New York, I was supposed to sing the national anthem on my own—and I went blank for so long I got booed at! It's probably a good thing we moved to England straight after."

"Yeah," said Michael. "Going blank is bad! But so is sweating . . ." Touching his forehead, he wiped away a big bead of sweat that had appeared.

"I don't want to go red," said Josie, touching her pale, freckly cheeks. "If my face goes red on television, I'll have to move to another country—like you did, Tom!"

I wished Josie hadn't reminded me that we were going to be on television too. Standing up onstage and talking in front of the whole school was scary enough, but knowing that lots of people would be filming us too made it feel ten times worse. Now that Ahmet was the Most Famous Refugee Boy in the World, millions of people had found out that we were going to Buckingham Palace for tea with the Queen, and a lot of reporters from the World's Press wanted to film our assembly for the news. So Mrs. Sanders was letting them—which meant we were probably going to be on every news channel in the country.

Mrs. Khan, who is the best teacher anyone could ever have, said we should try and pretend the reporters weren't there, and that would make doing the assembly easy. But I don't know how anyone can pretend something isn't there when it is. Especially when the something is real people with cameras who are going to be staring at you! It's always easier for me to imagine things *are* there when they aren't—not the other way around. My imagination isn't strong enough to make real things disappear.

Looking at Michael and Josie, I started to wonder which was worse—going red or going blank or sweating so much it looked like you'd been caught in the rain. I couldn't decide, so I told my brain to try not to do any of them.

"Did you all practice again at home yesterday?"

I asked. "I did and Mum said I was good but that I should stand up straighter."

Everyone nodded, except Tom.

"I tried," he explained. "I mean, I wanted to . . . but you know . . . brothers . . ."

Josie gave him a pat on the shoulder. Tom has more older brothers than should be allowed, and they never leave him alone. He has to share a room with two of them, and the main things they like doing are play-fighting and teasing him and stealing his food, which they do all the time. I've heard grown-ups tell Tom he's lucky to be the youngest brother. But I don't think Tom feels that way at all.

As the bus came to a stop and we got off and made our way toward the school gates, I told myself that everything was going to be fine. After all, Mrs. Sanders had told us exactly what she wanted us to talk about: why the Queen had invited us and what we were going to say to her. And Mrs. Khan had helped us write everything out and had let us stay in at break times all week to practice too. I had copied out our Ten Important Questions in my best handwriting so we could read them clearly. And Ms.

Hemsi, Ahmet's special teacher who could speak Kurdish just like he did, had helped him practice his part of the presentation in English so he could say why it was so special that the real Queen of England wanted to meet him.

There were only two things that could spoil any of it. The first was if one of us forgot to speak when it was our turn. But the second thing was even worse: and that was if Brendan the Bully decided to do something bad to Ahmet in front of the whole school and the World's Press. I hoped he wouldn't, but you can never be too sure with bullies. Especially not one who hated Ahmet so much that he nearly got expelled because of it.

2

The Revenge That Stunk

Brendan the Bully hates Ahmet. And me. And Michael. And Tom. And Josie. In fact, I think he might hate everyone, but he hates us the most, because a few weeks ago he got caught calling Ahmet so many horrible names that he nearly got expelled. It wasn't our fault that happened, but bullies don't care if things are your fault or not—they just need someone to blame. So Brendan the Bully blamed all of us, but he blamed Ahmet the most. That was why I knew I had to keep a close eye on him and make sure he didn't do anything to ruin the assembly or our trip to see the Queen.

When we got into school, we made our way to the classroom. Ahmet wasn't there, but as we were sitting down at our tables, he ran in and sat next to Ms. Hemsi, his special teacher, at the back of the class. I gave him a quick wave and he gave me one back.

After that, everything began to feel strange and normal all at the same time. Mrs. Khan started to call roll, just like she always did, but instead of everyone saying "Here, Miss," in bored voices, they all answered their names in a jumpier way than usual—as if they had ants in their pants that were making them shuffle in their seats and look back at the five of us. I noticed Brendan the Bully and his two best friends, Chris and Liam, looking back too. But instead of scrunching up their faces at us like they usually did, they were laughing and whispering.

Ahmet didn't seem to notice that everyone was looking at all of us, but Josie's face was now so red and blotchy that it looked like a pizza, and Michael was sweating so much that even his glasses were steaming up. He also looked as if he was having a competition with Tom to see who could touch his hair the most. Tom kept patting his bright blond spikes every few seconds as if to check they were still there, and Michael kept poking at his bubbly Afro as if wanting to make sure it wasn't melting. I could feel my ears burning and my heart thumping inside them as I waited for Mrs. Khan to finish the roll.

After what seemed like three years, she finally did, and told me and Ahmet and Tom and Josie and Michael that we could leave early, and that Ms. Hemsi could go with us too. We grabbed our notes and our royal invitations, and Ahmet grabbed his bright red backpack. It still smelled of old baked beans—even though his foster mum had washed the bag with extra-strong liquid detergent at least nine times. That meant every time Ahmet picked up his bag, he had to smell that horrible smell and was forced to remember the time when Brendan the Bully had poured huge cans of baked beans inside it, just to be mean to someone who was a refugee. I guess there are some bad smells and memories that not even liquid detergent can get rid of.

"How are you all feeling?" asked Ms. Hemsi as we hurried down the corridor toward the main hall.

"OK," said Tom, his voice sounding extra squeaky.

We all nodded in agreement, but I knew we weren't really OK at all. Only Ahmet looked as if he was actually happy and not pretend-happy. He was holding his invitation out in front of him carefully, as if it was made of glass, and smiling. I wondered if back in his school in Syria, he was used to doing lots of assemblies. Maybe before the war had started and he'd had to run away, he had stood on a stage and spoken to his whole school lots of times. I told my brain to remember to ask him later, or to ask Ms. Hemsi to ask him for me.

"Ah, there you are, kids! Good morning, good morning," cried Mrs. Sanders as we walked through the large double doors leading into the main hall. There were long lines of people with cameras standing in front of all the walls. Mrs. Sanders came over to us and made us walk quickly past the reporters and cameras that were now clicking and flashing and whispering at us. They made Michael so nervous that he tripped up the stairs and Josie nearly dropped her invitation, but they each pretended they hadn't done either of those things. We hurried to the side of the stage and stood behind the large, red velvet curtains that were hanging there. It felt good to get away from all the shining eyes and lenses, even though I knew they were waiting for us.

"Whoa," whispered Tom as he peeked out from behind the curtains. "I've never seen so many cameras! Not even when we first got famous!"

"They are here because the Queen, she is our friend now! Yes?" asked Ahmet, nudging me with his elbow and grinning.

I smiled back at him and then peeked out through the curtain too. I wanted to see if there were any reporters who looked like Tintin because if there were, then maybe they would be nicer to us than the reporters who had made up stories about us when we became famous the first time around. But there wasn't a single reporter that looked like Tintin. Not even by a little bit. Most of them were wearing smart suits and shiny shoes and looked like people who worked in banks and offices.

I'm pretty sure those kinds of reporters aren't very much fun. If I do ever become a reporter when I grow up, I want to be like Tintin and wear a raincoat and scruffy clothes and go on adventures with a pet dog named Snowy. Only, in my case, the pet will need to be a hamster or a parrot or a boa constrictor—or something else that I'm not allergic to, but which can still be clever and save my life when I need it to. And even though I can't have a dog, I still want to be as brave and as friendly to everyone as Tintin is. And I definitely *don't* want to be like one of the horrible reporters who pick on people.

Ever since Ahmet made us famous, I've learned that not all reporters care about being friendly or even about telling the truth. I know because they've called Ahmet things that I don't really understand but which I can tell right away aren't nice. Words like *fraudulent* and *illegal immigrant*—which are grown-up ways of saying they don't like him. Some of them even said mean lies about me and Tom too! But Mum says that we should feel sorry for bad reporters because lying makes their words empty, and one day no one will believe anything they say. I had never thought of words as things that could be full or empty before, but Mum's a librarian who's read at least fifty-nine thousand books, so she knows all about everything.

After a few minutes, I snuck another look and saw the hall doors opening and classes walking in to fill up the rows of chairs that were waiting for them like train seats.

Mrs. Sanders came running up the steps of the stage. "No need to be nervous," she said, peering at us over the top of her glasses. "You'll all be brilliant. Just remember to speak as loudly and as clearly as you can, and most important of all, to have fun!"

I could hear Michael gulping loudly, as if fun wasn't something he was ever going to have again, and Tom tapping his framed invitation against his knees. I wonder why teachers and parents always tell you to have fun when you're about to do the scariest and most least fun thing you could ever do!

"Let's practice one more time!" whispered Josie, her face now so red and so blotchy that she looked like a can of minestrone soup.

I nodded and, blinking my eyes so they would focus, got out our list of questions. I looked down at them and hoped they would help me remember everything I had to say.

The list looked like this:

THE 10 MOST IMPORTANT QUESTIONS TO ASK THE QUEEN OF ENGLAND (WHICH WE CUT DOWN FROM 52 ALMOST-AS-IMPORTANT QUESTIONS)

1. Have you ever met anyone who's more famous than you? (Tom)
2. What's your favorite football team? (Josie)
3. How heavy is your crown and does it give you a headache when you're wearing it? (Michael)
4. What's your favorite fruit? (Ahmet)
5. If you weren't the Queen, what would you have wanted to be? Would you have liked to be an astronaut maybe (because of all the star medals you wear)? (Me)
6. Who's the Lord Chamberlain who wrote our invitations, and can you do his job even if you have bad handwriting? (Tom)

7. How does it feel using money and stamps and things with your face on it, and do you like your picture or do you wish you could change it? (Josie)
8. Have you ever been to Disney World? And did you get to go on all the rides for free because you're the Queen? (Michael)
9. How many handbags do you have and which one would you take with you if you had to run away from a war? (Ahmet)
10. Will you help more children like Ahmet stay safe and find their families until all the wars end? (Me and everyone)

"OK, you lot! Ready?" asked Mrs. Sanders. And before any of us could shake our heads with a yes or a no, she stepped out onto the stage and, clapping her hands, shouted, "QUIET, EVERYONE!"

Instantly, the hall fell silent.

"Good morning, school!"

Everyone shouted back, "Good morning, Mrs. Saaaaan-ders!"

Mrs. Sanders nodded proudly and, clasping her hands together, looked out at everyone.

"Tomorrow, as you all know, five of your fellow students will be off to Buckingham Palace to meet the Queen and join her for what I imagine will be a rather wonderful tea!"

Someone cried out "Wooooohoooooooo!" which made everyone else giggle and laugh.

"Yes! Woooohooooo indeed," said Mrs. Sanders, smiling. "Now, Ahmet and his friends have been invited to meet the Queen because they did something extraordinarily brave and kind to help each other. And since we are a School of Sanctuary, which values acts of kindness and courage, I am sure you are all as proud of your fellow schoolmates as I am. So instead of my boring you with all the details, I'm going to ask them to come out to tell you all about it—and show you the messages they have received from the Queen!"

Everyone began to clap and cheer and whoop, and Mrs. Sanders waved us out onto the stage. My ears felt like they were full of cotton wool and my head was fizzing like a big ball of electricity as I followed Ahmet out and stood next to him. I looked out, but instead of seeing faces I knew, I saw an ocean of eyeballs blinking back at me.

"Ahmet, you're first. Off you go!" said Mrs. Sanders. She gave him a little pat and walked off to the side of the stage.

I watched as Ahmet looked over his shoulder at Ms. Hemsi, who was giving him a double thumbs-up. He took a step forward. Flicking his hair out of the way, he looked out at the school with his gray-brown lion eyes and opened his mouth.

"Tomorrow, I will go and I will see the Queen of England," he shouted. "Because she invite me to her house!"

He took another step forward and held up the invitation, showing everyone the message the Queen had sent him. His invitation was different from the rest of ours because, after his name, the Queen had written out *The Bravest Refugee Boy I Know.*

"In Syria, when we go to friend's house, we bring . . ." Ahmet stopped and tried to remember the word he needed. Everyone waited and I could feel my mouth wanting to yell the word out for him.

"GIFTS!" shouted Ahmet, suddenly remembering. "We bring gifts of . . . sweets . . . and chocolates . . . so we can share with tea! So, when I meet Queen, I will give her sweets with lemon so she can share. And I will show her this."

Ahmet lifted his backpack and held it up. I could see some people were frowning and whispering and looking confused, but they fell quiet when Ahmet opened his mouth again.

"This bag come with me from Syria . . . and it was GIFT from my dad. So I think Queen will like to see it and I will let her hold it so she can see everything inside it, and I will tell her to not smell it—"

"EEEEEEEEEEEEEEEEEEEEEEEEEEEWWW-WWWWWWWWWWWWWW!" screeched a girl from the back of the hall.

"UUUUUUUUUUUUUGHHHHHHHHHH!" cried a boy a second later.

"WHAT'S THAT SMELL?" yelled someone else from the middle of the hall.

The whole hall turned to look in different directions as people began to jump up from their seats with their hands over their mouths, squealing.

"STIIIIIIIIINK BOOOOOOOOOOOOMB!" came the answer from someone near the back, and instantly, everyone who hadn't already stood up jumped from their seats.

In less than a second, the whole hall had changed from a sea of eyes to a blurry rush of bodies running in different directions as teachers and children tried to get away from the disgusting smell.

But there wasn't just one disgusting smell! There were lots! Every few seconds, a new wave of terrible smells seemed to be coming from a different part of the hall. Mrs. Sanders had run back onto the stage and was trying to hold her nose and tell people to calm down at the same time.

"I'm going to die!" came a cry.

"We—got—a—get—ouwwa heeeeeere!" shouted a boy with his school sweater over his head.

"Miss! Miss! Look!" screamed a girl, pointing at the boy next to her who had begun to heave and howl as if there was a river about to burst out of him. "He's going to be sick!"

I knew me and Josie and Tom and Michael and Ahmet should have moved and run too, but we couldn't. It was as if our feet were superglued to the floor, and our eyes couldn't stop staring. It was strange watching everything from high up on the stage—even though we could smell the horrible smells, it felt as if we weren't a part of the school anymore and all we could do was stand and watch as everyone screamed and ran in different directions and crashed into each other like bumper cars.

"ORDEEEEEEEEEEEEEEEEEEEEEEEEEER!" shouted Mrs. Sanders, clapping her hands together and trying not to cough. From around the hall, we could see teachers pushing past the shocked reporters and frantically opening doors and windows.

"TEACHERS! TAKE YOUR CLASSES BACK IN AN ORDERLY FASHION TO YOUR CLASSROOMS! QUICKLY, PLEASE!"

Another stink bomb puffed into the air, making everyone squeal again—although now, some of the squeals sounded more excited and happy than shocked and disgusted. As the classes left, line by line, Mrs. Sanders hurried over to us.

"I'm sorry, kids, you'll have to get back to class—assembly is over, I'm afraid!"

"Oh!" said Tom, sounding disappointed. "That sucks!"

"We are not telling about this anymore?" asked Ahmet, looking at me. His lion eyes were getting bigger and bigger, and I knew he was feeling upset.

I shook my head, feeling sorry for him.

"No, I'm afraid not, Ahmet. Now off you go," said Mrs. Sanders, patting Ahmet on the arm gently.

Ms. Hemsi came to lead us out through the invisible clouds of smells. By now, most of the reporters were running out too. Some of them were even pushing past the classes in front of them to get out of the hall quicker.

As we left the stage and hurried out behind Ms. Hemsi, I felt a tickle at the back of my neck. Sometimes you can tell right away when someone is staring at you—it's like an invisible hand giving the back of your head a push. Sometimes the push can be a friendly one, but most of the time the push is a surprising and scary one—especially when the stare contains a bad feeling like the one I was getting right then.

So I looked over my shoulder. As I did, my eyes bumped straight into the bright, shining blue eyes of Brendan the Bully and I knew right away by the big smirky shape of his lips that he had done it! He had let off all the stink bombs somehow and had got his revenge on Ahmet by spoiling our special royal assembly. I didn't know how he had done it. He hadn't moved from his chair in the middle of our class row, and Chris and Liam had stayed next to him too, so he must have used something special to make the whole school stink. Maybe he had a super-special remote control gadget—or had people to help him on the other side of the hall! However he had done it, I knew I had to find out what else he had planned, and stop him from doing anything to ruin our tea with the Queen.

3

The Invisible Stinks

For the rest of the day, the whole school and everyone in it smelled of farts mixed together with the stink of old dustbins. But the smell wasn't nearly as bad as seeing Ahmet go quiet and sad. Josie and Michael tried to cheer him up by saying that the assembly didn't matter, because the Queen was still going to be waiting for us, and Tom gave him a sticker of a famous footballer at lunchtime, and I gave him all the lemon sherbets I had. But Ahmet still stayed quiet and sad, which made us all feel quiet and sad too. It didn't help that the school stunk so bad that it felt as if we might never be able to smell anything normal or nice again.

Our librarian, Mrs. Finnicky, was so disgusted by the stench everyone was carrying with them that she closed the library for the whole day—she said it was because she didn't want any of her books to smell as bad as we did and that humans were easier to wash clean than paper pages. And Mrs. Sanders did something that no one had ever heard of her doing in the whole history of the school: She canceled every single one of her after-school detention sessions. She said having to smell like garbage all day was punishment enough for everyone, and that it was her duty to the planet to make sure we all got home as quickly as we could so that we could take a shower.

But the person I felt most sorry for was Mr. Whittaker, the school cleaner, because thirteen people in the school were sick straight after the assembly. And as most of the people who got sick were the teachers, he had a lot more cleaning up to do than if it had been just us kids throwing up. Usually, no one ever saw Mr. Whittaker, but on this day, I saw him at least twenty times, running up and down the corridors with a mop and bucket and muttering angrily at everyone who passed by him.

"Man," said Tom, shaking his head as we all made our way out onto the playground at dismissal and heard a mop and bucket clanking past us. "I think Mr. Whittaker is going to need a holiday after today!"

"Yes," said Ahmet. "And new mop too!"

I grinned at Ahmet and gave him a thumbs-up. Now that he was beginning to speak English more and we could understand him better, his jokes were getting funnier.

"I hope we don't still smell tomorrow when we go to see the Queen!" said Michael, waving his arms up and down in the air as if that would help make the stench go away. But it didn't. Instead, it made him trip on his undone shoelaces. He would have fallen over, but Ahmet caught his arm and stopped him.

"Thanks, Ahmet," said Michael, pushing up his glasses. Michael never thanks any of the rest of us when we stop him from banging into things or falling over. He only ever thanks Ahmet, and it always makes Ahmet shrug and Tom give an almost invisible scowl.

"I see you tomorrow, yes?" asked Ahmet, spotting his foster mum waving at him through the school gates. She was wearing the same long red woolly scarf that she always wore, and today her blond hair was blowing around in the wind so much it looked like *it* was trying to be a scarf too.

"Yes," I said. "You are coming to my house tomorrow so that my Uncle Lenny can drive us to the Queen's!"

Ahmet nodded and, giving us all a wave, ran off to join his foster mum. We watched as he reached her and stood stiffly, like a soldier in an army, so that she could bend down to give him a hug. I guess he always stood like that because she wasn't his real mum and he was still waiting for his real mum to come and join him. His foster mum never seemed to care. She always hugged him and ruffled his hair anyway. But today, as she was hugging him, her usually smiling face began to frown.

"Ooooh, I think the stink's gone up her nose!"

whispered Tom. Ahmet's foster mum quickly stood up straight, and taking a step back, shook her head and made a funny noise with her throat—like a goose choking on a peanut.

"Someone should have warned her," said Tom, shaking his head. "As soon as I get home, I'm going to tell everyone to hold their breath until I've had a shower. Especially Dad! He's got asthma! One sniff of me and it could finish him off!"

"Guys . . . what if we *do* still smell this bad tomorrow?" asked Josie. Grabbing her braid, she tried to pull it close to her nose so she could smell it. "Ugh!" she cried, wrinkling her freckles. "It doesn't even reach and I can smell it! The Queen might throw up! And then she'd have us arrested!"

"Wait! Maybe THAT was his plan," I exclaimed, giving Tom a punch on the arm. Tom rubbed the spot and looked at me, confused.

"What plan?" asked Tom. "Whose plan?"

"You know," I explained. "Brendan the Bully's! He was the one who set off those stink bombs, I know he was. What if he stink-bombed the *whole* school not *just* to ruin the assembly but so we smelled so bad tomorrow that the Queen's guards would stop us from seeing her!"

Josie, Michael, and Tom stopped and stared at me with their mouths open. After exactly two seconds, they all shook their heads.

"Nah! Brendan the Bully's not that clever!" said Tom.

"And we don't know for sure that it was him!" said Josie.

"I agree," added Michael, frowning. "We shouldn't think it was him right away just because we don't like him. Mum's always saying we shouldn't cloud our brains with bad judgments, or the wrong person gets blamed and put in jail. We have to see the evidence."

Tom and Josie nodded in agreement, because Michael's mum was a lawyer who was always rescuing people and trying to make people's judgments act fair again.

I looked around the playground to see if Brendan the Bully was close by. Maybe if they could all see his smirky lips, they would know I wasn't being unfair. But I couldn't see him anywhere. Instead, I saw Jenny, who ran the school newspaper—with a crowd gathering around her!

"Come on! There's Jenny," I said, grabbing Josie's arm and dragging her after me. "She might know more about what happened."

We ran over and joined the whispering crowd standing in a circle around Jenny. As the school's news reporter, Jenny spies and listens and tells everyone everything about what's going on in school. The only problem is, she's not a very good reporter, because her stories often have lots of bits in them that aren't true. But because she mixes them up with things that *are* true, no one can tell the difference, except the person the story is about. Most people just believe her because it's easy and they don't have to think so hard about it.

"What's she saying?" asked Tom, leaning in.

A boy in front of us, who was from the year below us, looked over and whispered, "She says she knows who the stink bombers are! But she can't tell us their names because they're a part of a gang."

"No waaaaaaaay," whispered Josie as Jenny began to speak even louder so everyone could hear her.

"Yeah! An *international* gang! And TODAY was the day they wanted everyone to know they're real!" shouted Jenny, grabbing her two long braids and twisting and untwisting them around her hands like smooth, brown snakes. "There's one of them in EVERY school in the world now and that means every school is gonna get stink-bombed one day. But they picked OUR school first and they picked today because they knew the reporters were going to be here and because we're already famous because of that Ahmet kid!"

"What's the name of the gang?" asked someone as we all huddled in closer.

"Yeah! And what's their symbol? Is it like a fart cloud?" shouted someone else.

"How come we've never heard of them before?" asked a girl standing in front of Michael.

Standing on her tiptoes, Jenny popped her head up above everyone else's like a submarine's eye to check for eavesdroppers and enemy reporters who might steal her story, and then, crouching back down, whispered loudly, "I'm not supposed to know this, but I'll tell you. The gang is called the

Invisible Stinks and their mission is to make sure that everyone is—"

"What's happening here, then?"

We all jumped away from Jenny as Mr. Whittaker's large, balding head and brown uniform broke through the crowd and loomed over us.

"Anyone been sick? Because if they have, they can bleeding-buckets well clean it up themselves!"

Everyone stared up at Mr. Whittaker in silence.

"Go on, then, off with you! If you're not puking your guts out, you should be getting yourselves home and cleaned up so you smell human again!" And, waving us away, Mr. Whittaker headed back into the school.

A car horn beeped across the air, making Jenny jump up and grab her bag. "I'll tell you more on Monday!" she shouted as she ran over to her dad's car.

"But we can't wait until Monday!" said Tom grumpily to us as the crowd broke up and we headed to the bus stop.

"The Invisible Stinks Gang could strike anywhere. What if they target the palace next?" asked

Josie, walking faster and faster so we would get to the bus stop before the next bus.

We boarded the bus home along with everyone else from school who needed to go in the same direction. After a minute or two, the grown-ups already on the bus started to frown, just like Ahmet's foster mum had done. Some of them held their noses shut with the tips of their fingers. Others shuffled in their seats and tutted loudly, trying to move their faces closer to the open windows. And after a few seconds, a dog began to howl. By the third stop, the whole bus was empty of anyone who wasn't from school.

"That was fun!" said Tom as he jumped off at our stop. "I think I might join the Invisible Stinks Gang if it means I can get a seat on the bus every day!"

"You do know that's not the name of a real gang, don't you?" I said, rolling my eyes. I couldn't believe that Tom had actually fallen for Jenny's story! "Jenny was making that up. It was Brendan the Bully who did it. I know it was! It was him and Chris and Liam punishing Ahmet for nearly getting them expelled."

"But they were all sitting together in assembly,

remember?" Josie reminded me. "And the stink bombs were coming from everywhere!"

"They got some other people to help," I said. "Other bullies in the school who don't like Ahmet."

"But no one *saw* them do it," said Michael, shrugging. "Not even you. So you can't be sure!"

But I *was* sure. And I was going to prove it. All I needed was a little help from the Queen . . .

4

The Story That Broke the Internet

The next morning, I jumped out of bed so hard my knees shook and the floorboards groaned. It was finally here! The day that me and my very best friends on the whole entire planet had been waiting for: We were going to go and meet the Queen! The real, live, *actual* Queen—the one we saw on our pocket money and in the newspaper and on the television and on stamps.

And just as soon as I realized it was here and that I had to get ready, I instantly felt sick. It's funny how your brain can be so happy about something that it feels as if it might burst into a billion stars at any moment, but your body can feel like it has the flu and is hot and cold and sweaty and giddy. As if there are two different people stuck inside of you, having a fight.

"Ah, you're up early!" said my mum, walking in with a huge smile on her face. Mum doesn't really smile very often—not properly—but when she does, it feels like magic and as if anything can happen.

Mum used to smile all the time when Dad was alive—even when there wasn't any real reason for her to smile. Like when Dad never read the signs properly and got lost driving us to an adventure and she had to read the maps properly for him, or when she had to eat another dinner that Dad had half burned without meaning to. Dad loved cooking and driving, but he was never good at them—even though he was a carpenter and could make whatever he wanted with his hands. I can remember Mum making fun of him and making him laugh too.

But four years ago, when I was six, Dad died in a car accident, which made Mum stop smiling. Now she only smiles when something extra special happens. So I want to make as many extra-special things happen every day as I possibly can. Some days it's hard. But other days are easier. Like the day you're about to go and have tea and biscuits and who knew what kind of cakes with the Queen.

Feeling too excited to do anything else, I ran and gave Mum a hug. But I was jumping up and down at the same time, so it wasn't as warm and cuddly as it should have been.

"Calm down, calm down!" laughed Mum as she stroked my head. "We can't have you hopping all over the place like a frog when you go to meet the Queen!" She gave my head a long sniff. "And you smell fine now, thank goodness! Go and wash up and I'll get breakfast ready, OK? You've got hours yet!"

I nodded and, still jumping up and down because I was too excited not to, went and got as clean as I could. I had washed out the horrible smells from my hair and nose last night, but I wanted to make extra sure I didn't smell even a little bit like stink bomb. So I scrubbed my face extra hard with soap and brushed my teeth for an extra minute and used three extra squirts of hand wash.

Then I ran back into my room and closed my door and stared up at the clothes Mum had hung up on a large hanger to make sure they wouldn't get creased. There was my most special black shirt with sparkling silver stars and golden planets all over it that Mum had ironed until it looked brand-new—even though it wasn't and I had worn it to at least four parties and even to Buckingham Palace on my last adventure there. But the Queen hadn't seen it that last time because of everything that had gone wrong, so it didn't matter. Then behind my shirt was a brand-new pair of black jeans that Uncle Lenny had bought for me—because he said going to meet the Queen was like going to a wedding, and that you should always wear at least one new thing. And tucked into the pocket of the jeans was an extra-special pair of socks that I had bought with my own pocket money. They were bright blue with little dogs all over them—because I read that the Queen likes dogs, and if I run out of things to say to her or if she starts to look sleepy and bored, I can show her my socks. It's good to have a backup plan.

I was in such a rush to get dressed that I banged

my arm on the door and stubbed my toe on the bed, but I was too happy and excited to feel any pain. I was pulling on my second sock when I heard the doorbell ring and Mum running to open it.

"There's my little tiger!" cried Uncle Lenny as I ran out of my room to see who it was. Uncle Lenny is Mum's brother. He has a mustache that tickles my face whenever he gives me a kiss on the cheek, and because he's a taxi driver, he likes putting his hands on my shoulders and pushing me around the flat as if I was a car. I was so glad that my horrible aunt Christina wasn't with him that I gave him a running hug too. Aunt Christina isn't nearly as nice as Uncle Lenny—no matter what's happening or how happy you might be, she always looks confused and angry at the same time, and sniffs the air as if her nose is hunting for clues.

"All spruced up and ready to go, I see!" said Uncle Lenny, holding me away with his arms extra straight so he could see all of me at the same time. "You look as if you're fit to go see a Queen! Oh, wait a minute! You are!" Uncle Lenny looked at me for a second and then began to laugh so much that a tear fell out of his eye. Then, shaking his head, he muttered, "Ah! That was a good one!"

Grown-ups always like laughing at the things they say—even when what they're saying doesn't seem even a bit funny. It's very strange, but then, most grown-ups are. Even Uncle Lenny sometimes.

Mum brought me a bowl of oatmeal with a small mountain of strawberry jam in the middle and Uncle Lenny switched on the TV. Usually, I wasn't allowed to have breakfast on the sofa and watch TV too, but it was such a special day that it felt like all the normal rules didn't matter anymore.

"Here, look," said Uncle Lenny, putting the volume up. "Your school's on the news again! I saw it last night too."

"Really?" I asked, feeling surprised. Mum had worked late at the library last night and Mrs. Abbey, our next-door neighbor who looks after me sometimes, had wanted to watch a program about people who tried to bake perfect cakes and then cried when they couldn't. So I had spent all evening reading my favorite Tintin comic books instead, and thinking about the different cakes the

Queen might be asking her bakers to make for us, and how I could convince her to help me prove that Brendan the Bully was a Stinking Criminal. I didn't think reporters would care about Ahmet and the assembly because it was canceled, so I hadn't watched the news at all.

As I took a bite of my oatmeal, and Mum took a bite of her toast, and Uncle Lenny took a sip of his coffee, the newsreader on the TV peered out at us with a serious look on her face. Behind her was a picture of my school hall—it showed everyone frozen right in the middle of running and screaming and looking extra panicky.

"Newham's Nelson School is once again at the center of a scandal that is rocking the nation," said the newsreader.

"What? Because of the *stink bombs*?" I asked, wondering how stink bombs in an assembly could rock a whole nation.

"Shhhhh," said Mum, putting down her toast. Mum only ever put food back down on her plate when she was serious or angry, so I put down my spoonful of oatmeal too.

The newsreader, as if she had been waiting for us to be quiet, continued. "Yesterday, stink bombs disrupted the school as it gathered for a morning assembly, leading some to wonder if the act was a protest against the impending meeting between Her Majesty the Queen and Ahmet, the refugee boy who made headlines a few weeks ago."

"It wasn't a protest against that!" I cried, feeling angry. "It was just Brendan the Bully being stupid!"

"Shhhhhhhhhhhhhhh!" ordered Mum again, leaning closer in toward the TV.

"Ahmet was made famous for inspiring a group of children from his class to attempt a break-in at Buckingham Palace. Their aim was simple: to obtain the Queen's help with locating his family—an act which sparked headlines and inspired the Queen to invite Ahmet to tea. In a special address to his school, Ahmet was due to give details about his forthcoming visit but was cut short by a flurry of stink bombs, leading to a mass evacuation of the premises and many children and teachers falling ill. Now it seems that what was thought to be merely a childish prank may have actually been part of a wider protest taking place on the streets of London. Here is Ramesh Djai with the full story."

The picture on the television changed from the newsreader to a video of our school hall. I could see Ahmet and me and Josie and Tom and Michael, all standing on the stage, looking very small, and Ahmet's mouth moving, and then a puff of gray-green smoke and everyone running and screaming and pushing each other away.

But the screams were silent, because over the video, there was a man's voice saying: "Yesterday morning, hundreds of pupils were forced to flee from the assembly hall at Nelson School, after a co-ordinated stink bomb attack. Caught on film by the press, videos of the event are now going viral. The scene was one of pandemonium and chaos, with many asking: Was this a protest staged by students who disagree with the presence of refugee children at their school?"

The video of school was paused, and the picture changed again, this time to a tall, gray-haired man standing in the middle of a long, red road. I recognized the road right away—it was the exact same road me and Tom had walked down a few weeks ago to get help for Ahmet and his family!

"I'm here this bright Saturday morning in front of Buckingham Palace, where in just a few short hours, the Queen is due to meet with a child who might be the most famous refugee on the planet—a boy we all know as Ahmet." The reporter frowned as if the name Ahmet was so serious it deserved a special frown of its own. The frown went deeper as he said, "It's a meeting that has sparked endless debates, with some saying the Queen is overstepping her neutral position as head of state by welcoming a refugee of war to tea, and others arguing that supporting refugee children and families falls within the confines of her role."

The camera suddenly pulled away and turned left from the reporter's face. Right behind him, you could see a group of people holding up large signs and shouting angrily. Their signs said things like IMMIGRANTS NOT WANTED and GO BACK TO WHERE YOU BELONG! and REFUGEES NOT WELCOME. Lots of them were wearing big blue stickers that said FRY FOR PRIME MINISTER!

But opposite them, on the other side of the road, was another group of people with signs that said REFUGEES WELCOME and FOR QUEEN AND ALL COUNTRIES and ALL AHMETS WELCOME!

The camera went back to the reporter. Only now, the reporter wasn't alone anymore. There was a man standing next to him. A man with large black eyes and a dark gray suit and a bright blue tie. He was someone I had seen before and who Mum hated so much that seeing him now made her slam down her plate on the coffee table with an angry bang.

Uncle Lenny looked down at me and gave me a wink, which instantly made me feel less scared.

"Joining me now is Member of Parliament and leader of the National Union of Great Britannia party, Mr. John Fry," said the news reporter, holding out a microphone. "MP Fry, what do you make of the anger being directed at what is, to all ends, just an innocent tea party between the Queen of England and a ten-year-old boy?"

Mr. Fry smiled and looked at the camera, which caused Mum to make an angry growling noise with her throat.

"Innocent?" he asked. "Manipulating our monarchy for political ends is anything but innocent. Refugees leave their countries to take things that aren't theirs to take—whether that's jobs or homes or places in our schools or space in our hospitals. And, were I Prime Minister, I would have advised the Queen against meeting with these five highly dangerous children."

"Dangerous?" asked the reporter. He looked at the camera and then at the MP as if he was beginning to feel uncomfortable. "Surely you can't view these children as dangerous?"

"Yes. Dangerous. Any group of children willing to break the rules and attack the Royal Guards as these children had planned to do just a few weeks ago, are *highly* dangerous. And I am not the only one who thinks so. The protesters who let off the stink bombs in these children's school yesterday clearly feel the same—the whole thing STINKS. Refugees should NOT be—"

"That's quite enough!" said Mum, picking up the remote control and turning off the television.

"Couldn't agree with you more," said Uncle Lenny.

Then, giving me a nudge with his arm, he said, "We don't need no small *fry* ruining our day with the Queen now, do we?" And, laughing again, he wiped another tear away as I stared and wondered what was so funny this time.

I glanced over at Mum, who was looking at Uncle Lenny too and shaking her head and grinning. I wanted to ask her at least five questions about how we were going to get to the palace when there were so many people there and what if the Queen got upset and didn't want to see us anymore, but just then the buzzer to our flat rang. Mum jumped up and pressed the special camera button, then cried, "Come on up, Josie!"

Over the next hour, our flat went from just having me and Mum and Uncle Lenny in it to having me and Mum and Uncle Lenny; Josie and her mum and dad; Michael and his mum and dad; Tom and his mum; and Ahmet and his foster mum. Which, for a very small flat, was quite a lot of people and quite a lot of noise!

But everyone was so happy and looked so nice that it didn't seem to matter that no one could sit down. Everyone had worn their very best outfits: Ahmet was wearing a bright blue suit and a white shirt and a bow tie with dots on it and he had his red backpack with him; Josie was wearing a pair of sparkly overalls over a long-sleeve white top that had tiny yellow crowns all over it, and a brand-new pair of football shoes; Michael was wearing trousers that he said were made of tartan from Scotland, and a white shirt with a tie that matched his trousers; Tom was wearing a vest that shone blue and green at the same time, and a dark blue T-shirt that had a picture of a Lego Queen. I think he had put extra gel in his hair today too, because it looked stiffer and more golden yellow than it normally did.

Mum and me had spent all of last night cleaning and tidying and polishing and putting our books straight to make the flat nice for everyone, instead of watching a film or reading an extra-long story together like we normally did on Friday nights. I was glad it looked so nice, and I was especially glad I had tidied up my room, because it was the first time Ahmet and Michael and Tom had seen it.

I mostly only have books in my room and a table

filled with some of Dad's old pens and tools, but the one super-cool thing I have is the old-fashioned record player Dad left me. I played a record on it for everyone, and for the first time in a long time, it didn't seem to make Mum sad. I think she knew Dad would have liked everyone listening to one of his songs together.

"It's eleven o'clock, kids. Time to go!" announced Uncle Lenny, opening the front door and standing beside it like a butler. "Won't do to be late for the Queen, and traffic is never a friend to anyone on a Saturday!"

I looked around at my friends and gave them a massive grin. It was finally time to go and see the Queen and ask her our Most Important Questions! And no one—not Mr. MP Fry, or the people with the angry faces and signs, or Brendan the Bully's stink bombs, or even videos that were breaking the internet—could stop us.

5

Missed Directions

"In you hop!" said Uncle Lenny, opening the back door to his shiny, black cab. I love Uncle Lenny's cab because it feels like a mini limousine—it looks small on the outside but has enough space to fit seven people inside it—and at least five suitcases too. And it has lots of buttons and windows and slots and lights as well, so at night it feels like a spaceship. I could tell right away that it had been cleaned especially for today, because it smelled like cleaning polish.

"This is first time!" Ahmet smiled as he jumped

into the cab behind me. "In home, taxis they are white!"

I suddenly wondered what taxis in different countries of the world looked like, and if they were all like mini limousines too.

"Are you sure you don't want me to come?" asked Mum, patting my hair and smoothing my shirt for the tenth time.

I nodded. I secretly wished the Queen had invited all our parents and Ahmet's foster mum and Ms. Hemsi and maybe even Mrs. Khan to tea too, but she hadn't. Instead, she had said there were going to be two special guards to meet us at the entry door, and that whoever was with us could wait in a waiting room. I didn't want Mum to come to the palace and not be able to go in with me. It would feel worse than it did saying bye to her from outside our home. So we both agreed she would stay behind.

"DON'T SPEAK UNLESS YOU'RE SPOKEN TO, DARLING!" shouted Tom's mum as she shut the door after us. She gestured to Uncle Lenny to buzz down the window, and continued, "REMEM-

BER! SHE'S THE QUEEN OF ENGLAND! NOT YOUR AUNT MACY!"

"Michael? Michael! REMEMBER! Do NOT ask the Queen about how you can access the MI6 building!" cried Michael's dad.

"Ahmet—don't make the Queen smell the backpack, OK, darling?" said Ahmet's foster mum, waving. "Just show it to her."

"Remember to have fun, kids!" Josie's dad smiled.

Her mum started to cry, muttering, "Can't believe my baby's off to see the Queen! Never in all me life!"

I looked at Mum and waited for her to say something. But she just pushed up her glasses and gave me a wink. As if to tell me that no matter what I did, she would be waiting to hear all about it when I got home. The wink made me miss my dad and made my nose tickle, so I winked back with both my eyes, one after the other.

"Seat belts on?" asked Uncle Lenny.

We all gave him thumbs-up.

"Good, good! Then off we go!"

As we swerved away from the pavement and

waved bye to our mums and dads, Michael, whose seat was facing the back, twisted around toward Uncle Lenny's special glass window and shouted, "MR. LENNY, SIR, CAN YOU PUT THE METER ON?"

"Michael, mate, you don't need to shout!" said Uncle Lenny, laughing. And then looking into his special mirror, he frowned at us through his reflection and asked, "Why do you want the meter on?"

Michael shrugged and said, "So I can watch the numbers go up and see how much money it would have cost if we were paying."

Uncle Lenny laughed again, and, tipping his cap, he said, "Aye-aye, Captain!" and switched on his money box. That's the box that every taxi has that counts how much a driver is owed. In most taxis the numbers are red, but I told my Uncle Lenny that it looked scary—like the numbers that you see on bombs in big action movies—so he managed to change the colors for his box to yellow.

Michael watched for a moment until the numbers changed from £2.50 to £3.00. Then he gave a big sigh and smiled, looking happier than I had ever seen him.

Taking a journey in a black taxi from one part of London to another is fun when you're on your own. But when you're with your very best friends, wearing your most favorite clothes, and the driver happens to be the greatest uncle ever, it feels like the most exciting journey in the world. Even the boring parts of the city that you see every day change shape and become shiny and new—as if they secretly belong to a brand-new city that you can only ever see when you're sitting behind a different window. We all giggled and pointed and poked each other in the arm as Uncle Lenny drove us past houses that got bigger and redder and taller, and shops that shone with more and more lights. The numbers on Uncle Lenny's meter got higher and higher until it reached exactly £52.40, and the cab slowed down and came to a stop.

"Hold up . . . what do we have here, then?" asked Uncle Lenny, looking around.

I looked out our window and shook Tom's knee.

I knew where we were! We were near the palace! Up ahead were the huge arches crossing the large red road that we had walked through just two weeks ago—when we had been on a completely different and far scarier adventure.

Someone tapped on Uncle Lenny's window. We all leaned over to see who it was. It was a police officer with a helmet on her head and dark brown eyes.

"Sorry, sir, but you won't be able to turn here," she said, pointing in the direction of a long line of police who were standing across the road. "There's a protest, so the road is blocked."

"This is like the last time!" whispered Tom, looking worried.

"I see that," said Uncle Lenny. "But these children here have an appointment with the Queen."

The police officer tilted her head to one side. "Have they, now?" she asked.

We all nodded as Ahmet pulled out his invitation to show her. Pushing it to Uncle Lenny through the slot where people usually put their money, he said, "It is real—from the real Queen!"

Uncle Lenny handed the police officer the invitation. She read it, smiling a little bit.

This is what Ahmet's invitation looked like:

The Lord Chamberlain is commanded by Her Majesty

to invite

Ahmet Saqqal,

The Bravest Refugee Boy I Know,

to a Special Afternoon Tea

at Buckingham Palace

on Saturday, 27th October, at noon.

THIS CARD DOES NOT GUARANTEE ADMITTANCE.

"They're meant to be at the East Gate in ten minutes," explained Uncle Lenny, looking at his watch nervously.

The police officer nodded and, turning away from us, started speaking into the walkie-talkie that was taped to her bright yellow police jacket.

"What if they don't let us go through in time?"

whispered Josie. Grabbing the end of the braid her mum and dad had made her put her hair into again, she tried pulling it to her mouth.

"Here you go," said the police officer, poking her head through the window and giving Ahmet back his invitation. "You can head on down to the East Gate—but you're going to have to leave the cab here, I'm afraid. The crowds are a little too thick for a vehicle to get through, so instead, Officer Jensen and Officer Wu will be escorting you." She pointed over her shoulder to two officers in bright yellow jackets and waved at them to join us.

"All right," said Uncle Lenny. "Where shall I park?"

"Just leave the vehicle here," said the police officer, pointing to a spot right beside her. "And Mr. Ahmet Saqqal?"

We all looked at Ahmet as Ahmet looked up at the police officer.

"It's a pleasure to have met you." And with a tap of her helmet, she smiled and waved us through the long line of officers standing behind her like a human wall.

Ahmet went bright red and, smiling with all of his face, put his invitation carefully away again in his backpack.

"Come on, kids, we best hurry!" said Uncle Lenny as he parked the cab and Officers Jensen and Wu joined us. Officer Jensen was very tall and pale and had almost as many freckles as Josie, and Officer Wu was skinny with shiny black hair, and had a frown that was as deep as a miniature ditch on his forehead.

"Right, kids, looks like we might have to run!" said Officer Jensen as Uncle Lenny swung open the car door and grabbed my hand. I jumped out and everyone else leaped out behind me.

"Join hands and don't let go," instructed Officer Wu, walking in front of us. "Follow me, please!"

We all joined hands and began to walk as fast as we could down the large red road toward the palace, looking like a short and bobbing snake. Both Officers Wu and Jensen kept on waving at us from the front as they shouted, "Make way, please, make way!" to the crowds around us.

But as we got closer and closer to the large

black gates of the palace and the huge water fountain that lay in the middle of the road, it got harder and harder to see Officer Jensen—even though he was so tall, or to hear Officer Wu. There were so many other police officers everywhere and so many people with cameras and bags and signs, and so much noise, that we kept on having to let go of each other's hands and quickly join up again to make it through the crowd. But then, even that got harder to do too.

"Try to keep up!" cried Officer Wu as Uncle Lenny let go of my hand and waved at us to walk closely in a line behind him instead. But the crowds were getting taller and squashier and louder, and within a few seconds, I couldn't see the top of Uncle Lenny's head anymore or Officer Jensen's helmet or Officer Wu's bright jacket. All I could see were people's coats and trousers and shoes. And all I could hear were people shouting about refugees and how they were welcome and how they weren't.

I looked behind me to make sure that everyone was still there, but all I could see was Michael pushing up his glasses and struggling to keep up with me. I turned around to tell Uncle Lenny to ask the officers to slow down—but he was gone!

That was when I heard someone shout, "LOOK! IT'S HIM! IT'S THAT REFUGEE KID, AHMET!"

Instantly, everyone around us turned to look and shout and point. I stopped and hopped around to try and see where Ahmet was to make sure he was OK. Michael joined me and then so did Josie and Tom—but we couldn't see Ahmet anywhere.

And just then someone else shouted, "HERE! THOSE ARE HIS FRIENDS!"

The crowd around us shuffled and pointed and stared at us as cameras clicked, and my breath began to feel squashed. Some of the faces around us were frowning and angry and they were holding up the horrible signs I had seen on the news. They got closer and closer, pinning us into the middle of a circle, when suddenly, Josie gasped. I looked over my shoulder in the direction she was staring and saw what had made her go so white.

Through a small gap in the crowd, I could see Ahmet, who was standing about ten steps away. He was nearly surrounded by another crowd. But he wasn't alone. He was staring up at a man, and the man was holding Ahmet's red backpack, as if he was trying to stop him from running away. I knew right away who the man was by his dark blue suit and the golden ring he was wearing on his little finger. It was MP Fry!

But it wasn't seeing him that made me suddenly feel as if my hands and feet had frozen. It was seeing the man next to him. A man with a long face and long nose and long lips and a large brown bristly mustache . . .

It was Mr. Irons—the strictest, most horrible, most hated teacher who had ever taught at our school.

Michael and Tom had seen him at the same time. They gasped as Josie cried out, "What's HE doing here?"

We all stared at Mr. Irons. He had helped Brendan the Bully get away with hurting Ahmet! And now he was here, smiling down at Ahmet as if he had just been given the world's best birthday present, and making my insides feel like jelly and fire all at the same time.

And without thinking or being ready or knowing what I was doing, I felt my legs push against the ground, and my arms push everyone around me away and my voice cry out, "YOU LEAVE HIM ALONE!" and for a few seconds, everything seemed to stop.

I had reached Ahmet and MP Fry and Mr. Irons, and heard the footsteps and breaths of Tom and Josie and Michael as they came up behind me. I reached out and touched Ahmet's arm so that he knew I was there with him. My heart was marching through my head, and my stomach felt like it was an ocean full of crashing waves, but I didn't care. We stood and stared up at MP Fry and Mr. Irons and all the people around them who were staring back at us, and waited for whatever was about to happen next.

But as we waited, from somewhere in the distance, a clock struck twelve. Something heavy dropped into the ocean in my stomach and sank to the very bottom. Because I knew right away that we weren't ever going to get to the Queen on time, or get to ask her our Ten Most Important Questions.

6

The Lord of Chambers and Lions

Sometimes, the quietest people can surprise you—especially when they get angry.

I knew that because I had seen Ahmet fight bullies when he had never even spoken two words in English, and I had seen Mum yell at a man who was being horrible to a woman on the bus, when she never usually yells and instead tries to "bite her tongue." I can't bite my tongue because it hurts too much, so I always say what I think most times. So do Tom and Josie. But Michael never says anything when he gets angry or upset—he goes quiet and looks as if he's thinking a Deep Thought or waiting for someone else to speak up for him.

So, standing there in front of MP Fry, who was still holding on to Ahmet's bag, nobody expected Michael to say the things he said. In fact, I don't think even Michael expected it, because his face looked so surprised and confused afterward.

This is what Michael shouted: "YOU GIVE AHMET HIS BAG BACK, OR I'M GOING TO FIGHT YOU AND SUE YOU AND MY MUM WILL TAKE YOU TO COURT FOR BEING A—A BAG SNATCHER WHO SNATCHES BAGS FROM REFUGEE CHILDREN! SO GIVE IT BACK NOW OR ELSE!"

When he had finished, I could feel Michael shaking next to me and I heard Tom whispering, "Whoa!"

Then, from somewhere in the crowd on the other side of the road, a man shouted, "YEAH! YOU GO, MY LAD!" and a woman cried out, "SHAME ON YOU, FRY! SHAME ON YOU, FRY!" And within a few seconds, lots of people were shouting out the exact same thing as the woman. I looked across the road to where they were all standing and saw the nicer signs that I had seen on the news that morning. I realized that we had been trying to push through the horrible crowd to get to the Queen's palace, when we should have gone through the opposite side!

That was when I saw Uncle Lenny and Officer Jensen and Officer Wu pushing their way through the crowd toward us, looking red and sweaty and hot. Officer Wu was shouting something into the large walkie-talkie on his shoulder that sounded like "Backup! Backup! Center point 312!"

"Are you all OK?" panted Uncle Lenny, quickly checking our faces with his eyes.

I didn't answer, because MP Fry had grabbed Ahmet's bag and was raising it up in the air. It was clear he wanted to say something. Uncle Lenny stood behind us with his hands on mine and Ahmet's shoulders. It felt as if he was our bodyguard and as if nothing in the world could ever hurt us. The crowds slowly became quiet as the police officers and the cameras and reporters pushed closer, making MP Fry's smile wider. I didn't like seeing Ahmet's red backpack in MP Fry's hands, because I knew how important it was to Ahmet and how badly he had wanted to show it to the Queen. But I made myself stay still and wait, because I knew I was too short to reach it.

As MP Fry began to speak, half of the crowd began to boo and hiss while the other half cried out, "Darn right!" There was a pounding in my ears, just like a drum beating, so I couldn't hear any of his words except "Queen and country" and "duty."

All around us the crowds seemed to be getting bigger and taller, so I held on tighter to Ahmet's arm. I could tell he was getting angry because he was beginning to stand more stiffly and his hands were curling up into fists—just like they had done when he had roared at Brendan the Bully on the playground once. But I knew we were safe because now a lot of other police officers had joined Officer Jensen and Officer Wu, and all of them were busy trying to make the crowds stay back and not squash us.

I looked up at Mr. Irons and saw he was still

smiling at us, as if seeing Ahmet upset made him happy. MP Fry was smiling too, so much that it was as if his teeth had taken over most of his face. He was waving at the people behind us, and looking at the news cameras.

Then, suddenly, he raised his hands a second time. The booing and hissing and cheering instantly became quiet again as he took a step back and cried out, "But don't just take my word for it! Mr. Irons has firsthand experience of just how dangerous allowing refugees into our country and our schools can be!"

I felt my own mouth fall open as Mr. Irons stepped proudly forward and took Ahmet's bag in his hands. I could hear Ahmet growling like an angry lion and felt Josie taking a step forward as if she wanted to kick Mr. Irons in the leg just as hard as she could. Everyone around us was now looking at Mr. Irons, waiting to hear what he was going to say.

Mr. Irons puffed up his chest and, stroking his mustache, looked at the cameras. He had just opened his mouth, when suddenly—

SCREEEEEEEEEEEEEEEEEEEEEEEEEEEEEECH!

Everyone jumped and turned as the largest two gates of the palace began to slowly squeak open.

A hush fell over the crowd as all the cameras and reporters and crowds turned away from Mr. Irons toward the gates to see what was happening. After a few seconds, the gates clanged to a stop, and two of the Queen's special guards with their large pointy swords and giant black hats marched from their huts at the front of the palace right up to the corner of each gate, and gave a salute.

As soon as their fingers had touched their hats, two police officers on motorcycles appeared from the back of the palace, followed by a large black shiny car with two flags fluttering on the front fenders. The flags were golden yellow and red and blue, and showed dancing lions and a harp.

Almost immediately, whispers and shouts began to fill the air.

"It's the Queen!"

"It's her butler!"

"It's the royal baby!"

"Quick! Take as many photos as you can!"

"Make sure you're rolling!"

The police officers in yellow jackets began to wave the crowds back against the walls so that the car could come through the palace gates and out onto the road. Even MP Fry and Mr. Irons were forced to move to the side next to the Queen's large water fountain.

I looked at the car and its dark windows and wondered if the Queen had become so angry with us for missing tea and making people argue outside her house that we had made her leave the country. I wished I could have made her understand that it wasn't our fault, and that we had tried our best to get to her on time.

We watched as the car slowly rolled out of the gates and then headed toward the fountain. But instead of passing it by and continuing up the red road, it stopped. Right in front of us!

Ahmet grabbed my elbow and I grabbed Michael's as a door swung open. Everyone gasped as we waited to see who it was, hoping it would be the Queen.

But it wasn't. It was a man. A very tall, tanned

man with brown-and-white hair, dressed in a black suit and wearing the largest golden necklace I had ever seen anyone wear in real life. He looked like he could be a mayor, but I knew the Mayor of London was a woman named Piya Muqit and I had seen what she looked like in the newspapers, so I knew it wasn't her.

Looking down at me and Ahmet and Tom and Josie and Michael, and bowing his head at Uncle Lenny, the man smiled and said, "I hear you are running slightly late for your scheduled meeting with the Queen?"

Josie nodded and opened her mouth. But instead of saying "Yes," she gave a hiccup so loud it seemed to echo across all of London. It made her turn so red that even her freckles seemed to disappear.

"Let me introduce myself. I am the Lord Chamberlain, and—"

"Whoa! You mean you're the man who sent us our invitations?" interrupted Tom.

The Lord Chamberlain smiled again. "And you must be Tom?"

Tom cried out "Whoa!" again and looked at me.

He poked Michael on the arm as if Michael might not have heard and whispered, "He knows my name!"

"And you must be Josie . . . and Michael . . . and Ahmet . . ." Holding out his hand to each of them in turn, he shook theirs. Then he turned to me and introduced himself to me and Uncle Lenny too and gave us a handshake that was as warm and as soft as a slice of freshly baked bread.

"As the Lord Chamberlain, I am responsible for overseeing all of Her Majesty's ceremonial duties—which includes looking after the very special guests permitted entrance onto her grounds and chambers. The Queen has taken note of the cause for your delay and has sent me to fetch you—if you would kindly permit me to do so?"

"You mean . . . we get to go in your car?" asked Michael, so excited that he was pushing up his glasses even though they didn't have anywhere left to go.

The Lord Chamberlain smiled and, stepping back behind the door, waited for us all to climb in.

"We are going to meet Queen, yes?" asked Ahmet, squeezing my elbow even harder.

I was too excited for words to come out, so instead, I nodded as fast as I could.

"Good," said Ahmet as he turned around and took three steps up to Mr. Irons. Putting his hands on his hips, he shouted, "You give bag back to me! The Queen—she needs to see it. It is come all the way from Syria and is gift from my dad!"

With his face crumpled like a sulking baby's, Mr. Irons slowly reached out and gave Ahmet his red backpack. His nose began to whistle loudly and angrily like a very faraway train, and some people behind him begin to mutter and whisper. But as soon as Ahmet had his bag back in his hands, a deafening cheer rippled through the crowd. I waited for the boos and hisses too, but there were none. The Lord Chamberlain had made them go silent.

Then, just as we were about to climb into the car, the Lord Chamberlain turned to MP Fry and, in a voice that was different and stricter than the one he had used for us, said, "Her Majesty wishes to convey a message to you, sir."

MP Fry stood up straight and held his nose high in the air—almost as high as Mr. Irons's.

"Yes?" he asked.

The Lord Chamberlain continued, his voice very loud and clear, "Her Majesty wishes to thank you for your concern regarding her position as the head of state; but she would like me to remind you that she has been in this honored position for longer than you have been alive. And as the longest reigning monarch in history, she would also like to remind you of the depth and breadth of her knowledge as regards her duties and limitations."

MP Fry looked as if he didn't know what to say, and behind him, reporters and cameramen and lots of people in the crowd giggled and whispered. And then, as if his teeth were trying to stop his words from coming out, he replied, "Please thank Her Majesty for her kind reminder."

The Lord Chamberlain smiled and, after making sure we were all seated safely in the car, calmly walked around to the front seat to sit next to the driver.

"I THINK MP Fry just got TOLD!" whispered Tom as the large black car turned smoothly back toward the palace, and another cheer rang through the air around us.

I grinned and felt Uncle Lenny give my hand a squeeze as the flags with the golden lions and the lord who looked after them led us toward all the Queen's grounds and chambers.

7

The State and Its Secrets

Meeting the Queen and eating finger sandwiches the size of really tiny fingers and thirteen different kinds of mini cakes, and getting to ask her all the questions we wanted to ask, and playing with her dogs, and holding the crown she likes to wear best because it's the lightest and doesn't give her a headache, made all of us so happy that I don't think we'll ever not be happy ever again. Even Uncle Lenny, who was allowed to meet the Queen for twenty whole seconds before being given tea and cake in her waiting room, said he had never known a day like it and that it would stay with him for the rest of his life.

I think as happy as she made us, we made the Queen happy too, because after Ahmet showed her his bag and we all helped explain why it was so important, and he had asked her his questions about wars and handbags, and we had all asked our last question about how she could help other children like Ahmet too, she said she had never been asked questions like them before, and that she was proud of us for being brave enough to ask them.

But she also told us that everything she said in the palace was "off the record"—which meant that everything she said needed to stay a secret. Even if it was something as small as knowing what her favorite fruit was! I guess it's because the Queen doesn't want anyone to record what she's saying in her own house, as it's where she has to do all her State work and her Home work too. So when we got back to school, and Mrs. Sanders told us we were going to do another special assembly so we could tell everyone about our visit—to make up for the assembly that had been stink-bombed—we didn't have anything new to say! We couldn't tell anyone what her answers to our Ten Most Important Questions were, or what her dogs' names were, or what cake she liked to eat best, or if she wore a wig or not, or if she liked the picture on the money and coins we used—even though we knew the answers now. All we were allowed to talk about was what we had worn and what food we had eaten and how many different cups of tea we had, and how many times I sneezed because I had forgotten I was allergic to dogs—even the Queen's ones. And about how much Ahmet had loved telling the Queen about his bag and his mum and dad and sister Syrah—and how the Queen hadn't minded smelling the bag at all! After that second assembly, Ahmet was still famous, but I think his red backpack became even more famous, because now that everyone knew the Queen had smelled it, they wanted to smell it too.

And even though I couldn't share any of the Queen's secrets with Mum or Uncle Lenny, they didn't mind, because they got to share in all the things that happened straight after!

Things like MP Fry being forced to resign the very next week! And all because some people with whips in his party said that they didn't like how he had treated Ahmet and his red bag, and how he had insulted the Queen. I didn't know people in Parliament carried whips with them, but I guess that's why so many of them have briefcases. And I guess once you've been whipped, you can't go back, because MP Fry was never heard from again.

That same week, Mr. Irons also tried to tell his story on the news, about how Ahmet was the one to blame for all the changes at our school, and how he was costing the school money because he needed extra help from people like Ms. Hemsi. Mr. Irons even tried to say he had lost his job because of these things and that Ahmet was to blame for everything that had happened to him. But then the reporters talked to parents from the school and found out the truth about why he didn't have a job anymore, and how he had been a bad teacher, and after just two interviews, he disappeared too. I hope we never have to see him or his mustache or hear his whistling nose ever again!

And the very next week after that, my guess that Brendan the Bully was behind the stink bomb attacks was proven right! Well, nearly right.

Because there had been lots and lots of videos taken by the World's Press at the school on the day of our first assembly, someone had found one that showed who had set off all the stink bombs. Brendan the Bully, Liam, Chris, and six other students were all caught! But even though the cameras had caught them, no one could figure out who was the leader, so instead of one person being punished, they all got a month's detention and were never allowed into assembly again without having their pockets checked in front of everyone. I still know deep down that Brendan the Bully was the leader, because none of the other bullies cared about hurting Ahmet as much as he did. But he hasn't come after Ahmet or any of the rest of us since.

I was glad because I had asked the Queen to help me find proof, and I knew she would. I guess she must have asked her special guards and officers to make the World's Press check their cameras again; otherwise, Brendan the Bully might never have been caught.

And something else happened because of the day we met the Queen. Something that feels more important than anything else—even us knowing secret secrets! And that's the Very Big Debate that is happening in Parliament right now! Every day, for two whole weeks, Mum has been bringing the newspaper home and letting me stay up late to watch the news on TV and try to understand it all. And at school, me and Josie and Tom and Michael and Ahmet have been asking Mrs. Khan and Ms. Hemsi to help us learn about it too.

The Very Big Debate is a word fight—like the one we saw outside the palace. Except this one is between MPs and doesn't involve any signs. MPs are debating to see if they can keep the border gates open so the whole country can help refugee children like Ahmet stay safe from wars and be with their families. I don't know what's going to happen, but now I know that some of the most powerful people in the country care and want to help, and Mum says that's a good start.

Mum also says that the Queen isn't the one who made the Very Big Debate happen, because she's not allowed to tell MPs what to talk about or what to do. But I don't think queens and kings always need to *tell* people what to say or do to show that they care.

Sometimes they can show that they care in other ways.

Like by mailing a very special handwritten invitation. Or by sending a car with lion flags to come and rescue you when angry people are shouting. Or by hosting a tea party in their palace, where they give you finger sandwiches the size of really tiny fingers and thirteen different kinds of mini cakes, and they tell you and your best friends all the State Secrets, and also let you show them your socks.

THE GREAT FOOD BANK HEIST

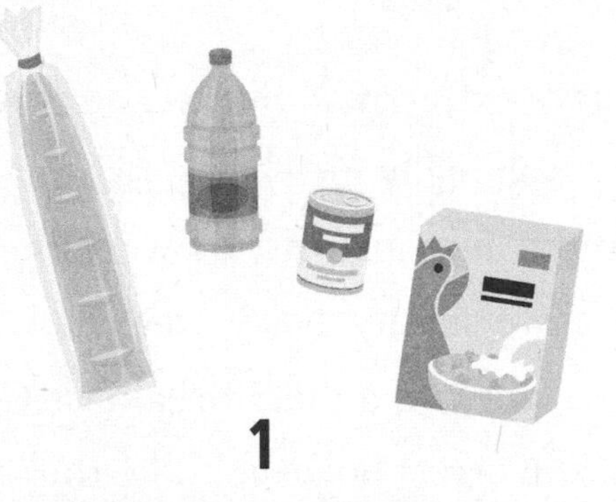

1

Just One More Day . . .

"Nelson, I'm hungry! I can't wait anymore. Look—my tummy's gone in!"

I looked at my sister, Ashley, as she lifted her T-shirt and sucked her tummy in just as hard as she could. She knew I hated it when she did that, because it looked horrible—as if her tummy was being sucked down a hole.

"All right, all right!" I said, putting down my pen and getting up from the living room floor. I would have to finish my homework later.

I was hungry too. School dinners never filled me up anymore. For some reason, the dinner ladies always gave extra-small helpings on the days when the food was really nice—like fish finger and fries days. And was it just me, or were the fish fingers getting more skinny every week, as if all the fish in the sea were on a diet? Breakfast Club was still OK, but the cereal boxes felt like they were getting smaller too . . .

Ashley stomped into the kitchen with me, her ponytail swinging from side to side. She was hugging her favorite toy of the week. This week it was one of my old plastic cars, which she had decided to call Freddy. No one knew why.

She jumped up onto her favorite chair at the kitchen table, patted Freddy, and then looked at me hopefully.

It was time again.

Time for me to play the Pretend Game.

The Pretend Game was when I had to pretend we had food left in the house even when we didn't.

I hated playing the Pretend Game. Out of all the games I had to play at home, it was the worst one. Especially when it was coming to the end of what Mum called "A Really Tricky Month." That's a month when the money Mum got from her job wasn't enough to pay for food as well as for everything else we needed. But this month we were lucky. Someone had given Mum some vouchers, and I knew that tomorrow we would be heading down to the best bank in the world to cash one of them in.

"Hmm," I said as I went over to the fridge and opened the door wide.

The fridge lit up with a warm yellow glow, as if it wanted to show us that it had something inside for us to eat. But the shelves were empty, apart from half a jar of jam, a plastic bottle of mustard that had been there since before I was born, one egg, and a tiny bit of milk.

I could have boiled the egg for Ashley, but I knew Mum probably hadn't eaten all day at work, so I wanted to save it for her.

"Nope, nothing interesting in there," I said, closing the fridge door. "Let's try here!"

In the cupboard next to the fridge, there were packets of spices and salt someone at the Bank had once given us but which we had never used, a bottle of oil, and half a box of cornflakes. I could have given Ashley cornflakes, but I needed to save the milk for when Mum came home and wanted a cup of tea.

I shut the door, then opened the next one, and the next one, and the next one. And the whole time, I pretended there might be something inside to eat—even though I could have told Ashley what was in every single cupboard with my eyes closed.

I wished they were filled with food like my best friends Krish and Harriet's cupboards always were. When I grew up, I was definitely going to have cupboards like they had.

"We have to wait for Mum to get back," I said to Ashley. "She'll be here soon. Maybe she'll have picked something up on the way home."

"But I'm really, really, reeeeeeeally hungry," said Ashley, lifting her T-shirt and getting ready to suck in her tummy again.

But before she could do it, I grabbed the toy car and ran off with it.

"FREDDY!" Ashley shouted, and ran after me. I didn't really want to play, but I knew if I kept Ashley busy, she'd forget she was hungry. At least for a few minutes.

As I held Freddy high in the air and watched Ashley jump up and down like a human rabbit to try to grab it, we heard the sound of keys in the door. Mum was back!

"Kids?"

"Mummy!" squealed Ashley. She forgot about Freddy, ran to Mum and hugged her tight.

Mum smiled as I poked my head out the living room door. I only looked after Ashley for half an hour every day when we got home from school, but it always felt like ages.

"All right, all right, my little hugging machine," laughed Mum as she gave Ashley a kiss on the top of her head. I could tell Mum was tired, because her eyes were puffy. That meant she had had to work extra hard.

Mum worked as a nurse in a hospital, looking after lots of sick people who had just had serious operations. She had to take their temperatures and measure their heartbeats and make sure they had taken their medicines on time.

"Mum, I'm HUNGRY and Nelson hasn't given me or Freddy ANYTHING to eat," reported Ashley.

Mum looked over at me and gave her sad smile. I hated that smile. That was the other thing I wished for—even more than I wished for all the kitchen cupboards to be full. I wished I would never have to see Mum's sad smile ever again. The one that tried to hide how bad she felt about us not having enough to eat—even when she worked so hard and barely ate anything herself.

"Well, come on, then, let's see what magic we can find," said Mum. She gave me a pat on the cheek and hugged Ashley as we walked into the kitchen.

After looking through the cupboards just like I had done a few minutes ago, Mum shook her head.

"Just one more day," she promised as she took out the egg, the tiny bit of milk, the jam, and a can of kidney beans that was right at the back of the bottom cupboard. "Then we can go to the Bank and get the things we need. But for now, it's time to do a bit of magic with the things we have . . ."

As we all sat down to a dinner of a tiny omelette, a bowl of heated kidney beans, and a dessert of cornflakes dipped in jam, I felt my stomach swirl and growl. I crossed my arms on top of it to stop it from making any more noises and whispered to myself the thing that Mum had just said.

"Just one more day," I said as softly as I could. "And then you can have everything you need. . . ."

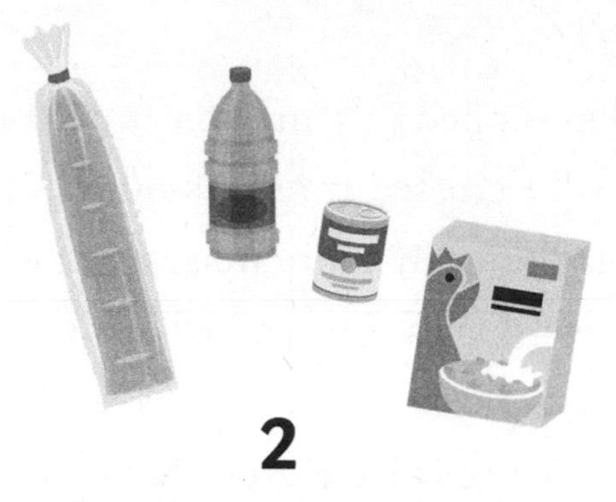

2

The Greatest Bank in the World

The next morning, I woke up extra early and jumped out of bed.

Whenever it was a Voucher Thursday, Mum always finished her shift early and picked up me and Ashley from school so we could go straight to the Bank with lots of shopping bags stuffed into our pockets.

Our Bank—the one we always went to at the end of a Really Tricky Month—was *the* best, *the* most fun, and *the* greatest bank in the world.

That's because our Bank wasn't anything like any of the boring old money banks you see on the main street, which are always gray and have big machines that swallow up cards and spit out bits of paper at you, and which are filled with gray-looking people who are always bending over bills and coins.

Our Bank—the food bank—was full of people in bright clothes who always smiled and asked us how we were doing. They were so kind and funny that they even made Mum forget about being embarrassed and ashamed about having to go to the Bank to get us food. Mrs. Patel and Mr. Anthony and a girl called Natasha—who had hair as thick as a horse's tail!—were my favorite bankers. We'd known them for nearly a whole year. Ever since Dad left us to go and make a new family that he wanted to be with more than with us.

I wished every bank near us was like the food bank. No other bank in the world had shining tins and rustling packets of delicious food stacked from the floor to the roof. No other bank let you take things out without you putting money into it first. And no other bank had a sign by the front counter that said MONEY NOT WELCOME HERE. It was the only place in the world, I think, that didn't like money. I wished the man who owned our flat and took rent money from Mum was like our Bank. He was always asking for more money—he never had enough to make him happy.

I picked up my school backpack, took out my Homework Diary, and flipped it to the back page. There, in extra-light pencil so that no one would see, was my Bank Withdrooling List.

My Bank Withdrooling List was a list of every single thing I had ever wanted to withdraw from the Bank and bring home for us to eat. You know, things that make your mouth go all watery and your tummy start to lick its lips and drool too!

This was what I had on my list so far:

BANK WITHDROOLING LIST

1. Choco loco Nutty Melts
2. Chocolate spread
3. Cheese and onion chips
4. Fizzy cola pop
5. Pizzas
6. Fish fingers

7. Frozen french fries
8. Chocolate cookies
9. Things to make in the microwave so I don't have to cook
10. Jelly roll (for Mum)
11. Butter (real butter, not the fake stuff in a tub)
12. Something green like peas so we can be healthy
13. Emergency pasta for when we run out of stuff
14. Kinder Eggs

When it was a Really Tricky Month and I got so hungry that I thought I might fade away, I loved looking at my list and dreaming that I had all those things to eat right away.

Nobody knew about my list. Not even Mum, or Krish or Harriet—even though they were my best friends. It was embarrassing making lists about food you wished you could eat when everyone else was making lists about computer games and toys that they wanted for their birthdays and Christmas and Eid and Diwali and other special days.

It was my Golden Goal to bring all the things on my list home from the Bank one day. It hadn't happened because normally the food the Bank gave us was serious—like bread and baked beans and potatoes and Weetabix. There weren't any fun things like chocolate cookies or chips. But Mrs. Patel always gave me and Ashley some treats as well, so for at least the week after a visit, we knew we'd have some chocolate.

Getting out a pencil, I closed my eyes and imagined what I would be eating right now if I could. The picture my mind came up with made my stomach drool extra hard. So I wrote it down:

15. Chocolate muffins

Then I snapped my Homework Diary shut and got ready for school just as quickly as I could. I was never, ever late for Breakfast Club, and today I wanted to be the first one there.

3

Breakfast Club

There was one rule to being a member of Breakfast Club and that was you never talked about Breakfast Club. At least, not with anyone who didn't go to Breakfast Club.

Our Breakfast Club at school was one of the best because Mrs. Bell and Mr. Ramjit ran it. Mrs. Bell was our head teacher and Mr. Ramjit was her deputy.

Mrs. Bell was always super strict about Breakfast Club. Everyone had to get there by 8:00 a.m. and be sitting down by exactly 8:05 a.m., and everyone had to choose a piece of fruit and a drink, and have one bowl of cereal and a piece of toast with one kind of spread on it.

I always chose a banana for my fruit if there were any left, any cereal that had chocolate in it, and chocolate spread or jam to go on my toast. Sometimes I wished I could have four pieces of toast and not just one. Especially on a Monday, when we hadn't had enough to eat at the weekend.

On Fridays at Breakfast Club, everyone got a treat! Nobody ever knew what the treat was going to be because Mrs. Bell bought it the night before with her very own money. The best treat was donuts or cookies. The worst was cold cups of yogurt! But none of us really minded. The most exciting thing was trying to guess what it might be.

I always tried to get to Breakfast Club super early because I didn't want Krish and Harriet to see me going into the hall for it. They were lucky and had lots of food at home, so they didn't need to go to Breakfast Club.

Krish, Harriet, and I did everything together—except Breakfast Club.

Krish was the shortest—and skinniest—boy in

our whole year. He wanted to be a spy when he grew up. I thought he would be good at it because he was so skinny that he could hide behind a lamp-post if he needed to and the bad guys would never see him!

It was funny Krish was so skinny, because he never stopped eating. His pockets were always full of sweets and mints and football stickers, and he always had the best haircuts because he copied the styles of our favorite footballers.

Right now, our favorite footballer was Noah Equiano—the whole world called him the Equalizer because he always leveled any game he played in before he scored the winning goal. And the best thing about him was that he was born in our town and had gone to a school only twenty minutes away! Me and Krish kept telling our parents to transfer us to that other school, but they said we didn't need to go to the same school as Noah Equiano to be as good at football as him. Parents don't know anything sometimes.

Harriet wasn't into football as much as me and Krish. She loved car racing and was always talking about circuits and lap times and horsepowers. She liked Equiano, but only because he came from our town. She thought Desiree Chadwick was much better because she was the first woman to win a Formula One Grand Prix in over forty years. Harriet loved arguing with us and wanted to be an inventor when she grew up. She was extra super-clever, so both me and Krish thought she could definitely become one.

I wished Krish and Harriet didn't know that I was hungry a lot of the time, but they did. We never talked about it, but they still knew. And I wished I could play with them in the mornings instead of having to go to Breakfast Club, but I needed Breakfast Club to get the energy, so I pretended I didn't come to school until later and I never told them about it.

"Morning, Nelson," said Mr. Ramjit as I walked into the hall.

"Morning, sir." I grinned as I walked past him and grabbed the first banana I saw.

"Your favorite's in today," said Mrs. Bell, giving

me a nod. "Chocolate hoops," she whispered as I grabbed a box. It wasn't every day we had chocolate hoops! I was so hungry I could have eaten ten boxes, but I didn't try to sneak another one and just went quickly over to Maureen, the dinner lady, to get myself some toast.

"What'll it be this morning, Nelson?" she asked, holding a knife between the chocolate spread jar and the jam jar.

It was an important question, so I took a moment to work out what my stomach really wanted. It growled loudest at the thought of chocolate spread, so I chose that.

"Good lad," said Maureen, nodding so hard it made her curly gray hairs look like they were having a disco but nobody else could hear the music.

I sat down in the spot I liked best, which was at the back of the hall. I ate the banana as quickly as I could and then reached out for the milk jug in the middle of the table.

"Hey, Nelson!"

"Hey, Lavinia!"

Lavinia came and sat next to me. She had bright orange hair that always looked as if it had been electrocuted.

Lavinia didn't say anything else. She chewed on her food slowly and gave a loud gulp every seven seconds, then looked over at everyone in Breakfast Club like a giant, human owl.

"Hey, Nelson, what do you think Mrs. Bell's gonna get us tomorrow?" asked Leon as he gave a silent nod to Lavinia and then filled his mouth with an enormous bite of apple.

I shrugged. "Chocolate muffins?" I said hopefully.

"They're way too expensive!" said William as he sat down next to us. He made sure Mrs. Bell wasn't looking, then licked the jam on his toast with the tip of his tongue, just like a lizard.

"Those things are like a pound for each one," William went on. "She can't afford that! Dad says teachers get paid bupkes. I don't know what a bupkis is, but I know it's not a lot, so Mrs. Bell definitely can't afford chocolate muffins for all of us!"

No one said anything else. We all ate our breakfasts and watched as more members of the club came into the hall.

"Hey, you guys, did you hear that there's something wrong with the food bank?"

We all looked up at Kerry as she slammed down her tray and flicked back her long brown hair. Kerry was always late and loved talking loudly. She was in Ms. Potter's class two doors down from mine, and we could still always hear her.

"No," I said. "Why? What's wrong with the food bank?"

"I dunno. But Mum and Dad went last night, and Kwan's gran went the night before that, and it looks like they don't have as much food there as usual."

Kerry sat down and added, "Kwan's gran said the bankers think someone's stealing stuff, but they don't know who!"

"Whoa!" said William as he started to lick at his cereal with his lizard tongue. "Why would anyone steal stuff from a food bank?"

"Yeah," said Leon, gulping down his apple. "Especially when there's a real bank with actual money in it right next door!"

Kerry gave a shrug. "'Cause they must be really dumb, I guess. Mum says it's not right—it's not fair."

William shook his head. "We're lucky it's not happening at Breakfast Club too, then. Isn't it?"

We all stopped chewing and turned our heads to where Maureen the dinner lady was standing and looked at the big table of fruit and cereals next to her. It didn't look as if anyone would dare to steal stuff from her.

"It better not happen here," said Leon, chewing his apple extra fast.

"Yeah. Well, just in case, you better all eat as much as you can at lunchtime—because who knows?" Kerry warned as Mrs. Bell gave a loud clap to tell us we only had a few minutes left.

Right away, everyone stopped talking and the noisy hall fell quiet. All you could hear was loud slurps, and spoons banging on the bottom of bowls.

I ate my toast as quickly as I could. What if the Bank didn't have enough food for Mum and me and Ashley tonight? I put my arms over my tummy again as it gave an extra-loud and worried growl . . .

4

Games & Empty Bags

I was still worrying about the food bank when the bell rang for the end of the school day.

"Your mum's here!" shouted Krish, waving at my mum like she had come to pick him up instead.

"Awesome," I said with a grin as I saw Ashley speed toward the school gates. She was still hugging Freddy as if it was a teddy bear.

Krish and Harriet joined me as I headed toward the gates too.

"What game will you play with your mum today?" asked Harriet, giving me a nudge on my elbow with her elbow.

I looked over at her and grinned. "Mum's always coming up with new ones, so I don't know."

"Wish my mum would come up with fun games to play," said Krish. "But she thinks I Spy is hilarious, so that's the only game we ever get to play with her."

"Nelson's mum's the coolest," nodded Harriet as she sucked in her lips and made an opening and closing fish mouth. It was her favorite thing to do, and she did it so much that I don't think she even knew she was doing it most of the time.

"Yeah, I guess," I said, doing my best not to grin. Mum really was the coolest.

"Hi, Krish. Hi, Harriet," said Mum as she smiled at us.

Krish's light brown cheeks suddenly flushed so bright red it was like watching a traffic light change color.

Harriet covered a snicker with her hand before saying, "Hi, Ms. James."

"Hi," blurted out Krish.

"Nice to see you both looking so well," said Mum.

"Krish, you must have grown . . . let's see, at least three millimeters since last week!"

"You really think so?" asked Krish, trying to stand as straight and as tall as he could.

"Why don't you both come over on Sunday?" asked Mum. "It'll be nice for Nelson to have you at ours for once, instead of me dropping him and Ashley over at your houses all the time."

"Yeah! And can you bring lots of snacks too?" asked Ashley. "And then leave them? I like prawn cocktail chips the best! And chocolate Penguins—even though they're not really penguins."

Now it was Mum's and my turn to turn into traffic lights, because I knew both our faces went red at the exact same time.

"Oh, don't you worry about that," said Mum. "I'll sort out some snacks!"

"Nah, Ms. James, I eat TONS!" said Krish. "I love bringing stuff to yours. Mum always gives me stuff that she only lets me have for treats when you invite us round."

"Yeah, and we've got WAY too many prawn

cocktail chips at home," added Harriet. "Nobody eats them—they're like the worst ones!"

I looked at Harriet and didn't know what to say, because I had seen her eat three bags of prawn cocktail chips in one go and then lick the inside of the bags too!

"Ah—well, if you must," said Mum with a smile, giving my hand a secret squeeze. She was trying to make me feel better.

"Right, then, we better be off," said Mum. She took Ashley's hand and waved at Harriet and Krish. "Give your parents my love!"

Krish and Harriet waved back as they turned to go home too.

"So, what game shall we play today?" asked Mum as we began the forty-minute walk to the Bank. We could have got the bus, but Mum only let us do that if it was raining, because she needed to save as much travel money as she could.

On this walk, Mum decided to play the Spirit Animals Game with us, where we had to look at the people walking past and imagine what spirit animals they might be. Ashley pointed at anyone wearing something glittery and shiny and announced they were a unicorn, but I spotted someone who could easily have been a crocodile, and another person who was definitely a human bumblebee—mainly because he was wearing a yellow-and-black-striped sweater.

When we got to the Bank and had to wait for our turn, Mum played the Guessing Game with us. That was when Ashley had to guess what food we might get to take home that day. Mostly, she got it wrong because she was only six and only cared about chocolate cookies and sweets. But it was still fun to play.

And then, when Mum was sorting out our vouchers with Mrs. Patel and Mr. Anthony, and Natasha was getting us our things, me and Ashley played the Keeping Time Game. That was when we tried to guess what Natasha was getting for us by how long it took her to go and get each thing.

"Right, kids . . . Looks like there's a bit of a problem," said Mum as she came back from the counter with just two bags and not the four or five we got every other time.

"Do we have to wait longer?" I asked as I took a bag from Mum and looked inside. There was a loaf of brown bread that Ashley didn't like, a bag of rolls, and two cans of baked beans instead of the normal four.

"Seems the Bank is a little short this month," said Mum, taking a deep breath. "But that's OK. We can make do, can't we, my little troopers?"

Ashley didn't say anything, and I gave a silent nod. When Mum said "little troopers," we both knew it was going to be a hard month ahead. Even harder than normal . . .

Then I remembered what Kerry had told us at Breakfast Club about someone stealing food from the Bank!

As I watched Mum trying to pretend that everything was fine, I promised myself that I would find out what was going on. And make it stop.

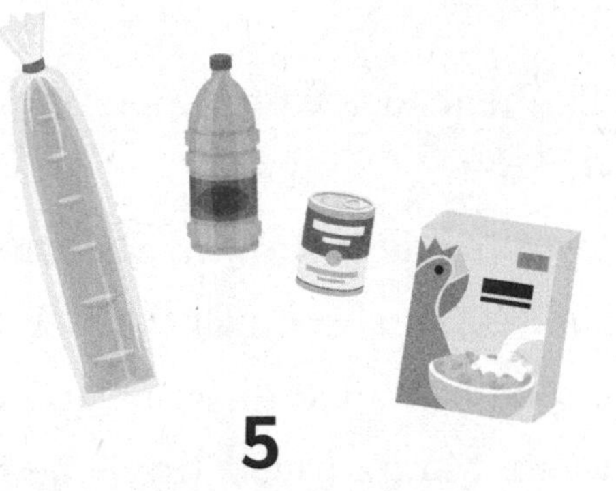

5

The Real Hunger Games

I hated the months when we had to be little troopers. They were always hard because the games we played at home suddenly didn't feel like fun anymore. Nothing was ever fun when you were so hungry you felt as if you were full of gaps and holes.

Normally the games we played made everything feel ten thousand percent better. And that was all because of Mum. She became a games inventor when Dad left us and she had to go to the food bank for the first time. She came home with some things we liked, and lots we didn't like at all. So to stop me and Ashley feeling as if we didn't want to eat the meals she made, Mum came up with all sorts of games.

My favorite one had to be Master Chef, which was when I got to choose all the weirdest ingredients the food bank had given us and cook a meal out of them. Mum's friend from the hospital had even given me a real chef's hat with a real burnt hole in it to wear when I was playing it!

So far, I'd come up with pickle hot dogs, tuna and jam pie, and noodles swirled with mustard and brown sauce. But the dish I was most famous for was Pineapple Surprise, which was bread soaked in lemonade and fried, topped with large, round pineapple slices from a can, and put in the oven so it looked like a burger. I'd never seen Mum's face look so funny as when she was eating that one!

The game Ashley loved best was the Menu Makers Game. We played that after every visit to the Bank. We made a list of everything the food bank had given us and then invented a proper menu—just like you get in a restaurant.

Ashley loved drawing and coloring in, so her menus were always the prettiest. When she did an extra-special one, Mum stuck it on the fridge. My favorite menu Ashley made was covered with pictures of mushrooms with salad leaves as wings, and fish with lots of fingers.

But there was one game we didn't really enjoy at all. Even Mum didn't like it, although she pretended she did. It was called the Transformers Game. We always played that in a Little Troopers Month, and sometimes we had to play it a few times.

It was where you looked at food that you didn't want to eat—not even a little bit!—and used your imagination to make it into something extra tasty and delicious, and then told everyone about it. Mum said she had invented it to help our imaginations grow stronger.

It was hard, but sometimes it did work. One time I transformed a horrible, lumpy, bright red sandwich filled with nothing but extra-squashy wet tomatoes into a huge roast chicken with a mountain of mashed potatoes with lots of butter melting down it like a volcano. I didn't have those things, but imagining them made me not mind eating the sandwich so much.

But in a Little Troopers Month, playing any of those games felt like hard work.

It was hard trying to make a menu when you didn't have much food to write out on it. And it was hard being a Master Chef when there weren't enough ingredients, no matter how nice and burnt-looking the hole in your chef's hat was. And it was especially hard when you had spent a whole day thinking about food—even in the middle of playing football or reading a book or trying to figure out your nine times table—and made yourself tired. At times like that, your imagination sometimes didn't want to transform something horrible into something better.

And sometimes none of the games worked at all, and everyone was just acting and pretending they weren't hungry when really they were so hungry that they couldn't sleep at night and cried when they thought no one else could hear them . . . Even Mum . . . Especially Mum.

6

The Last Pawn

At Breakfast Club that week, and the week after that, all anyone could talk about was the food bank and the fact that it didn't seem to have much food anymore.

Leon said the thieves had taken so many things that the Bank would need to shut down soon. But then William said that would be illegal and that the army would come to help and give us the sugar and tea and butter we needed, just like they did in World War Two. Kerry said that it didn't matter as long as we still had Breakfast Club and free dinners at school—except that maybe we would need to wear clothes with more pockets so we could save things to take home.

But as more weeks went by, things got worse. Mrs. Bell saw that we weren't talking or playing as much as we normally did, so she began to give out extra portions of fruit and toast. But it still wasn't enough. Nothing was big enough to fill the giant black holes in our tummies. Even Lavinia's red hair had started looking less electrocuted.

Krish and Harriet could see that I was feeling tired all the time, so they tried to give me food by pretending that they suddenly didn't like their favorite things anymore or had eaten too much already. I knew they were lying, so one day I told them to just stop it and to leave me alone.

"Stop what?" asked Harriet, looking shocked, while Krish stared at me with a cereal bar hanging out of his mouth.

"Just stop feeling sorry for me! I'm fine!" I shouted, feeling red-hot angry. "I don't want your stupid cookie!"

"I only asked if you wanted to share it with me!"

said Harriet, getting angry too. I could tell because her nostrils were moving up and down.

Krish was frowning and staring at me too as the cereal bar in his mouth began to crumble. Suddenly, I felt stupid as my stomach gave a roar so loud that everyone could hear.

"Sorry . . ." I said. "It's just . . ."

Krish slowly took a step toward me, as if I was a crocodile who might bite his head off.

"Did we do something wrong?" he asked.

I gave up. I knew I had to tell them, because if everyone at Breakfast Club was right, then me and Mum and Ashley were going to starve soon. In fact, we were already starving. This month felt harder than the last one. Last night we only had half a slice of toast each for dinner and Ashley had fallen asleep crying. Her insides were beginning to hurt again.

So I broke the Breakfast Club rule and told Harriet and Krish what everyone was saying about our Bank being robbed.

"That's horrible!" cried Krish.

"Why would anyone steal anything from a food

bank?" asked Harriet. She stopped being angry with me and got angry with the thieves instead.

I shrugged. "Don't know. But it means everyone just feels hungry all the time."

"Maybe the thieves are *selling* all the stuff they're stealing from the food bank," muttered Harriet. She shoved the chocolate cookie into my hand, and I gobbled it down as she carried on talking.

"But . . . how are they taking everything? Are they breaking into the Bank every night?" she asked.

I shook my head. The bankers had told everyone that no one had broken into the warehouse at all.

"Wait. Where does all the food for the Bank come from again?" asked Krish.

"From people at the supermarkets," I said. "They donate things and put them in a special shopping cart, and then the supermarkets take everything to the Bank. And then the bankers put the food on the shelves and give it to us."

"Cool," said Krish.

"Well, if it's not being nicked straight from the Bank, then the thieves have *got* to be stealing things from the supermarkets," said Harriet. "Mum and Dad always give our donations to Gladstores—the big one up the road. We buy extra stuff and put it in the food bank carts just like you said."

"Gladstores is the grocery store that gives my Bank all its food!" I said. I suddenly felt embarrassed—what if I had been eating food that Harriet and her mum and dad gave away to the food bank? Now I knew why Mum didn't like taking things from a charity. It was embarrassing to have to eat things that your friends had donated . . .

"Hey, maybe we should do a stakeout at Gladstores!" said Krish, getting excited.

"You mean a stakeout when you go and spy on people?" I asked.

"Yeah," answered Krish. "We could go undercover after school and find out how the robbers are stealing the food. If we catch them and take them to the police, maybe we could get a special medal too!"

"But how would we do a stakeout at Gladstores?" I asked. "It's HUGE! The thieves would be crazy to steal things with loads of people about."

"And don't they have a million cameras and security guards and things?" asked Harriet. "They'd have caught the thieves by now, wouldn't they?"

"Maybe," said Krish. He scratched his head and gave us a shrug as we all thought about what else we could do.

*

We soon forgot all about Krish's stakeout idea, but then something happened that made me so angry that I knew we had to do something.

The following weeks were good weeks because Mum got paid and could buy enough food with her own money to stop our stomachs from growling all the time. We were down to our last food bank voucher, and I knew Mum wasn't going to use it until she had to.

But then she did have to because the greedy rent man sent a letter telling us that Mum had to pay more rent or leave. After she had paid him, Mum had to take us to the Bank again right away. But when we got there, Mrs. Patel and Mr. Anthony and Natasha could only give us one and a half bags of food. They all said sorry a hundred times and looked so sad that it made me start to feel scared.

And then, the next week, Mum came home with the hugest bags of groceries me and Ashley had ever seen. They were filled with treats and bags of all the delicious things we loved but hadn't eaten in a long time.

There were chicken nuggets for Ashley, burgers for me, and french fries for us all, and Mum's favorite dessert—jelly roll!

It was as if Christmas had come, except there wasn't a man with a giant belly trying to come down a chimney we didn't have!

As Ashley skipped around the kitchen, singing, Mum turned on the oven and put in two burgers—one each for me and her—seven chicken nuggets for Ashley, and exactly thirty-three fries. I looked at Mum and frowned. Something was different.

"Mum, where did you get so much money from all of a sudden?" I asked as I helped set the table for what was going to be the best meal we had had in ages. I knew her payday wasn't for at least another week.

"Oh . . . just a bit of luck!" said Mum, giving me a wink.

And then suddenly I noticed it—the thing that was different . . .

It was the empty space on her finger.

"Mum!" I cried out. "Nan's ring . . ."

Heading over to the fridge, Mum opened the door and pretended she was looking for something inside it. My insides were getting too heavy, so I went and opened a cupboard door and put my head inside that.

We always ended up like that whenever I found out that Mum had paid a visit to the pawnshop.

When I was little, I used to think pawnshops had made a spelling mistake and that they sold prawns but had just forgotten to put the *r* in. But they hadn't, because they don't really sell anything at all. Not even prawns.

They let you borrow money in exchange for your most precious, most expensive things. And then, if you ever earn enough money again, you can go and buy your things back from them. But that never happens. Not for Mum anyway.

As I stood with my head in the cupboard, I made a promise that when I grew up, I would get a job that paid me millions of pounds and I would go and buy back Nan's ring just as quick as I could!

But for now, I wouldn't let Mum take any more of her things to the pawnshop. Nan's ring had to be the last pawn—ever! So as I waited for Mum to leave the fridge, I decided Krish was right. It was time to make a stakeout plan and catch the food bank thieves.

7

Stakeouts

The next morning at school, I told Krish he had been right and that we needed to do a stakeout.

"You mean it? Really?" asked Krish. He gave me a happy punch on the arm and started jumping up and down on the spot too.

"Let's do it today! After school," said Harriet, pulling us all together so no one could hear what we were saying. "We could run down to Gladstores—it's only a few minutes away!"

"But I've got Ashley, remember?" I reminded her. "AND I need to be home before Mum gets in."

"You can just come for a short while, then," answered Harriet. "And me and Krish can stay a little bit longer! Yeah?"

Krish nodded, and so did I. So right after school, we all ran to Gladstores. I told Ashley we were playing a special game and that if she was good, she could have something I had saved for her from my school dinner as a treat.

When we got to the supermarket, we tried to secretly spy on the food bank carts by walking up and down the aisles and watching the people who put things in the shopping carts. But we didn't see anything weird going on.

We did the same thing the next day, and the next, and the next. But all we saw were lots of people putting things *into* the food bank carts.

"This isn't working," said Krish, after we had been to the supermarket every day after school for nearly two weeks. By now the security guard was beginning to give us strange looks—he probably thought *we* were trying to steal something. "Maybe the thieves have kids, so they don't do any robbing after they've picked them up from school?"

"Maybe," said Harriet. "What we really need is a

whole day to try and catch them . . . I know! Why don't we try this Saturday?"

"Yeah," I cried. "Mum has to work on Saturday, so she'll be dropping me and Ashley off at yours anyway."

"Yeah, I know," answered Harriet, looking at me as if I was stupid. "That's why I said Saturday in the first place!"

"Cool," I replied.

"And that gives us a few days to plan and train hard so we can be super fast and sneaky and strong," added Krish. "I know all about that stuff, so I'll train you both. Deal?"

I nodded and so did Harriet. But then she added, "But I'll do the planning! So you have to listen to me about that. OK?"

Krish and me nodded, and over the next few days, we planned our big stakeout and did lots of training. Harriet drew out a plan on four pieces of paper stuck together with tape, and Krish trained us at break times and lunchtimes so we'd be extra fit and strong.

The training was mostly zigzag running through

the playground at top speed, just like Noah Equiano did on the football pitch, and doing karate chops and flying kicks, even in the middle of class. Everyone thought we were weird, but it was fun, so we didn't care.

By Friday night, we were ready.

On Saturday morning, after Mum had kissed me and Ashley goodbye, Harriet's mum took us upstairs to Harriet's room. Krish was already there, playing a computer game with Harriet as they waited for us—along with a mini mountain of food. That was the best thing about Harriet's house. There were always mini mountains of food everywhere.

As soon as Harriet's mum had shut the bedroom door behind her and we heard her head back downstairs, we all set to work.

I quickly packed all the food into mine and Ashley's backpacks. Harriet got four tubs of bright green and purple slime from under her bed and packed them into hers. She also switched on her speaker so that, together with her computer game, everything in her room sounded noisy and busy. Then she sneaked downstairs to get our coats. She made it back without being seen and helped me zip up Ashley's coat and explain to her that we were going on an extra-special secret adventure.

Krish had disappeared to the bathroom and suddenly came back into the bedroom, wearing a Spider-Man ski mask and carrying something red and sticky and wrapped in plastic in both his hands.

Everyone stopped what they were doing and stared at Krish with their mouths open. Even Ashley.

"Um . . . why have you brought ACTUAL steaks to a stakeout?" asked Harriet, her nose all scrunched up.

"Duh! There might be dogs," said Krish as he squeezed the two steaks into the back pockets of his jeans. "This will distract them. I got them from the shop next door to my house. But I can't touch them or anything because I'm Hindu and Mum and Dad will have a fit. It's disgusting even holding them! Ugh!"

Harriet turned to look at me with her mouth still open, but I understood Krish's point. "He might be right about the dogs," I said. "It's all right, Krish, I'll unwrap them and throw them for you."

Krish nodded, looking as happy as a Hindu vegetarian with meat in his pockets could.

"Anyway, why have *you* got a MASSIVE box of donuts and a thermos?" asked Krish, pointing at the box of twelve donuts and the thermos bottle Harriet was holding.

"Because that's what you have to eat on a stakeout—donuts and coffee. That's what they do in ALL the movies," she replied.

I grinned. When Harriet wasn't watching Formula One races, she was always watching cop dramas. Especially American ones. That might be why she had stolen her older sister's long brown coat that was too big for her, and a big hat. She was clearly trying to look like the detective from her favorite TV show.

"Got the plan?" I asked Harriet. I was starting to feel nervous.

Harriet nodded and took it out of her coat pocket.

We all looked down at it again. Harriet had

drawn in all the different aisles and where the food bank donation carts were. And, of course, where the security guard always stood.

Then, in glittery green, purple, and blue pen, she had drawn big fat arrows to show what we were all supposed to do.

"Here, take the whistles," Harriet ordered as she gave me and Krish a silver whistle each. "I've wiped them super clean," she added. "Mum's always leaving them all over the house."

Harriet's mum was a football coach, so she had at least five hundred whistles that she was always losing. She even kept some in her socks because she said that was the best place for a spare one.

"OK. Ready?" asked Krish. His voice sounded odd because of the Spider-Man mask.

We all nodded to each other and then looked down at Ashley.

"Remember, it's a secret, Ashley. We're going on a secret adventure, so you have to listen to me. OK?" I asked her. But she was so excited that Harriet was letting her take her hand that she didn't really listen to anything I was saying.

Sneaking out of Harriet's room, we all crept down the stairs and toward the front door. Harriet's dad was at his restaurant, so we didn't need to worry about him, but her mum and big sister were downstairs in the living room. Luckily, they were talking loudly on their phones and watching TV too.

"Quick!" hissed Harriet as she opened the door and rushed us all out. She closed it again very slowly so that only a small click could be heard. Then, waving to us all to copy her and crouch down, we ran past the living room window and out through the front gate.

"Phew!" said Krish as we got to the end of the road and stood up straight again. "That was easy."

"Again, again!" cried Ashley. She thought it was all a big game we were playing for fun.

"Later," I promised as we began to walk faster and faster toward Gladstores.

Gladstores was only a short walk away, but we felt nervous suddenly, and hungry too, so we each had a donut for luck and then tried the coffee. It was horrible!

As the sign for Gladstores got closer and closer, I could tell Krish and Harriet were asking the same questions in their heads as I was. Questions like: Were we ever really going to catch anyone—what if they were too clever for us? What if Harriet's mum or sister went up to Harriet's room and found us all gone? What if we didn't catch anyone at all and got into trouble anyway?

Then, suddenly, we were at the giant sliding doors of the supermarket and the huge sign that said WELCOME.

It was time for us to split up and try to catch a thief . . .

8

Supermarket Sweep

Harriet went inside first. She gave us a thumbs-up and a nervous smile and marched straight up the fruit aisle in her long coat and big hat. Her job was to watch the back exit doors, the ones with the long pieces of plastic on them that the supermarket workers always vanished behind.

Next it was Krish's turn. He waited until two people with a shopping cart walked past us, and then he walked after them as if he was part of their family. His job was to walk up and down the different aisles and see if he could spot anything fishy. Apart from actual fish, of course.

Then it was my turn.

I took Ashley's hand and went inside, heading straight for the magazine racks. From there, I could keep a close watch on the food bank donation carts, which were always parked between the newspaper stand and the red post office box right by the front door. Hanging from the ceiling was a bright green sign that said FOOD BANK DONATIONS.

I gave Ashley a comic about turtles to flick through and made her sit on the floor so that it looked as if we were waiting for our mum or dad. I watched the donation carts. There were three. One was very full, one was only half-full, and the last one was almost empty.

I watched and watched and watched the shopping carts as lots of people dropped things into them on their way out. Most put in all the normal things, like boxes of cereals and cans of tomatoes and packages of pasta. But some people put strange things in too: Like an old man who put in five packs of chewing gum and a bunch of flowers. And a woman who put in seven bags of red chilies and a basil plant.

"I don't want to read anymore," said Ashley, hugging Freddy and standing up. "I want to go back to Harriet's house and play!"

"If you read something else, I'll give you some chips," I offered as I took a bright pink packet of prawn cocktail chips from my backpack and held them out to her.

Ashley nodded and sat back down. As she crunched and gobbled, I gave her another comic to look through and went back to watching the carts.

And just as I was beginning to think that no one was stealing from the food bank at all, I saw it happen! The sneakiest of sneak attacks ever!

A man and a woman had stopped by the newspaper stand, pushing a shopping cart with just two packages of cookies and a bottle of water in it. They looked as if they were choosing a newspaper to buy, but then suddenly they were gone! They had switched their nearly empty cart with the food bank cart full of donations and now they were on their way out of the store with it as if it was theirs!

I blinked hard to check that my eyes had seen

right and then looked over at the security guard station—but there was no one there! The thieves must have seen that too! So I did the next best thing: I blew on my whistle just as hard as I could and pointed at the couple, shouting, "STOP! FOOD BANK THIEVES!"

The man and the woman looked back at me for a split second and then began to run out of the store. From somewhere behind me, I could hear Harriet and Krish blowing their whistles too, which meant they had heard me and were on their way—but they were going to be too late!

I snatched a cart that was standing next to me—I didn't care that it had some tins and boxes in it. Then I swooped up Ashley and her backpack, plonked them into it and ran after the thieves.

As I zigged and zagged and zoomed the cart past lots of other shopping carts, Ashley clapped her hands and giggled. But just as I pushed us out of the main exit doors, the alarms began to sound! My cart of unpaid food had set everything off!

"WHEEEEEEEE-WHEEEEEEEEEE!" cried Ashley even louder as I sprinted out into the car park.

From somewhere behind me, someone shouted, "OI! YOU KIDS THERE! STOP!"

I ran even faster, trying to see where the man and woman had gone—but there were so many people and too many cars . . .

A few seconds later, Harriet and Krish came crashing into me.

"Where . . . where . . . what . . . ?" asked Krish.

"Shopping cart switchers!" I tried to explain. "They—they switched a nearly empty cart for one of the donation ones! And they ran out here, but now I can't see them!"

"CREEPS!" shouted Harriet, hoping they could hear her.

"OI! YOU KIDS THERE! STOP!"

"Oh no! Security guard!" warned Harriet as we switched directions and began to run away from him too.

"Here! Take this!" I cried out to Harriet as I pushed the cart with Ashley in it over to her.

I jumped up onto the nearest shopping cart parking fence and tried to spot the thieves one last time.

"OVER THERE!" I shouted, pointing at a white

van parked in the back corner of the car park. "QUICK!"

I set off toward the van, running so fast that I couldn't feel my legs anymore. I could hear Ashley beginning to cry, but I couldn't stop. Just as I reached the van, the man and woman jumped into their seats and slammed the doors shut. We were too late!

"NOT SO FAST!" screamed Harriet as she and Ashley and their cart reached me. She ripped open her backpack, grabbed one of the tubs of slime and began throwing handfuls of it at the van just as fast as she could. In a few seconds, green splodges of oozy slime began to dribble and drool off the van's windows and doors.

The van jumped forward with a growl, making us all jump back a step.

"TAKE—THIS—ROBBERS!" panted Krish. He pushed his hands into his back pockets and pulled out the steaks. Pulling open the packet with a large "UGH!," he threw the meat toward the van's windscreen.

We watched as the two big red steaks flew

through the air and landed with loud thuds on the van's big front window.

"HA! Got you!" shouted Krish as a shower of chips and chocolate splatted onto the van windows and stuck to the slime. Harriet and I had taken everything we had in our backpacks and were throwing them at the van just as fast as we could.

"This is fun!" giggled Ashley as she threw chips and hungrily stuck some into her mouth too. I wished we could have taken all the treats home instead, but we had to stop the thieves!

"GET OUT OF THE WAY, KIDS! BEFORE I REALLY HURT YA!" shouted the man in the van as he rolled down his window and stuck his head out, before making the van roar again.

When we didn't move, the man switched the headlights on and shook his fist at us.

"You better move!" screamed the woman, rolling her window down too. "He doesn't like kids who damage his van!"

"Yeah! Well, WE don't like thieves who steal our food!" I shouted.

Harriet pushed the cart with Ashley in it out of

the way, and Krish ran off to the side as the van roared again and jumped forward.

But I didn't move.

The van roared again and again, and flashed its headlights at me like a giant monster.

But still I didn't move. Even though now I was getting scared.

The man behind the wheel was getting redder and angrier with every second.

"Nelson! Get out of the way!" shouted Krish as Ashley began to cry.

"NO!" I shouted back. "They're thieves! They're making other people go hungry! I won't move!"

From all around us, more and more people were beginning to stop to watch and listen. That was good, so I carried on shouting.

"THEY'RE FOOD BANK THIEVES! THEY SWITCHED THEIR SHOPPING CART AND TOOK THE DONATION CART!"

Inside the van, the man began to look around as if now he was the one getting scared. And the woman had put her head in her hands as if she wanted to hide.

"That's awful!" I heard someone say.

"That's shocking!" cried a lady. "Someone call the police!"

"Why's that van covered with slime and meat, Daddy?" someone else asked.

The van growled and roared again as the man inside shouted, "GET OUT OF MY WAY, KID! OR I'LL RUN YOU DOWN!"

A long, loud beep made me take a step back. But then someone suddenly stepped out in front of me.

It was an old man.

And a few seconds later, a younger woman joined him.

And then three men. And then Krish and another kid I didn't know.

They were all coming to stand in front of me so the van man couldn't hurt me!

"Exit the van with your hands up, NOW!" shouted a big man. It was the security guard that had been chasing after me and Ashley and Harriet and Krish just minutes before. He was sweating so much he looked as if he had just been for a swim.

"Come on! OUT! The jig is up!"

9

The Equalizer

After the security guard shouted out those words of warning, people came running from all directions. The supermarket manager and lots of supermarket workers wearing bright orange vests came running up to the van and shouted at the thieves to open the doors. And then suddenly, there were blue lights flashing and lots of police arrived too! All of them stood around the van as, at last, the man and woman gave up and came out with their hands in the air.

A police officer took their keys from them and opened up the back doors of the van.

Everyone gasped at the mountains of food stacked from the floor of the van to its roof.

"Whoa!" cried out Krish. "There must be fifty cartloads in there! They're PROPER thieves!"

"That's about right," said the supermarket manager as she turned to look down at me and Harriet and Ashley and Krish. We stood in front of her, our hands all messy with bits of chips and chocolate and blobs of slime.

"And you all helped stop them," the supermarket manager went on, her bright orange badge glinting down at us. It told us her name was Onioke Samuels. "Thank you!"

"Well done, kids," shouted the old man who had stood in front of me to protect me from the van. He walked up and gave me a pat on the back. "You were so brave! They would have driven away if it weren't for you!"

From somewhere at the back of the crowd, someone cried out, "Heroes! Those kids are heroes!" and began to clap loudly.

And before we knew what was happening, it

seemed everyone in the whole car park was clapping and shouting "HEROES!" at us too.

Ashley jumped up and down inside the cart excitedly as Krish turned bright red. Harriet waved at everyone like a queen and took off her hat to give them a bow.

"Kids, come with me, please," said a police officer as he began to steer me through the crowd and back toward the supermarket. "We've got some questions to ask you all."

For the rest of the morning, the police and the supermarket manager and then all our parents asked us what felt like a thousand questions.

At first Harriet's mum and then Krish's mum and dad and then my mum were furious that we had sneaked out of Harriet's house in secret. They had already been worried because Harriet's sister had found us missing, and when they were called by the police, they had felt sick.

They all said they were going to ground us for the rest of our lives. But when they found out we had wanted to catch the thieves because everyone at Breakfast Club was starving, and that we had spent days and weeks spying on the shopping carts and training and planning our stakeout, they all agreed that maybe they didn't need to ground us for that long after all.

Mum decided not to go back to work that day, and when we got home, she made me and Ashley two big cups of hot chocolate and asked us to tell her everything. Ashley pretended the cart had turned into a rocket ship and that she had thrown millions of sweets at the thieves. But I told Mum the truth. And about how I never wanted the food bank to ever be empty again, and how I never wanted me or Lavinia or Kerry or anyone from Breakfast Club to have to have holes in their stomachs all the time.

Mum didn't say anything. But I knew she was thinking of lots of things she couldn't find the right words for.

*

The next day, everything went back to normal. It was a normal, boring Sunday, when I had to do homework, and Ashley had to have the Sunday bath she always hated, and we all watched lots of TV.

But then on Monday morning, everything started to change.

First, a whole hour before I had to leave for school, the doorbell rang.

When Mum opened the door, a deliveryman was standing in front of her with a giant basket of food tied with the most giant orange ribbon she had ever seen.

The basket was filled with every kind of food you could ever imagine—cookies and popcorn and chips and sweets and fruits and cheeses and breads and bananas and . . . chocolate muffins!

"Who's it from?" I asked when Mum had screamed and made me and Ashley wake up and run to the front door too.

"Santa!" cried out Ashley.

But Mum shook her head. There was a small card tied to the basket, which Mum opened and showed me. "Read it, Nelson . . ."

Inside the card, in scratchy writing, were the words:

Dear Nelson and Ashley,

Thank you for catching the shopping cart thieves! We and all the food banks we support are eternally grateful.

Love from everyone at Gladstores XXX

"And here," said the deliveryman, smiling as he pulled something else from his back pocket and held it out to me. "This is for you too."

He handed me a folded-up newspaper.

I opened it—and gasped. There on the front page, above a huge picture of Noah Equiano, the best footballer in the world, was a giant headline that read:

SUPERMARKET GANG BUSTED IN FOOD BANK HEIST!

NOAH EQUIANO TAKES ACTION AFTER CHILDREN STOP DONATION THIEVES

I stared at Mum. She stared back and then gave me a hug so big I thought I could hear my bones creak.

After the deliveryman left and we all ate the best breakfast any of us could ever remember eating, Mum read the newspaper out loud to me and Ashley. It told us that the man and woman we stopped had been part of a huge gang who had filled three huge warehouses with food stolen from lots of different supermarkets. They had been swapping donation carts with emptier carts from supermarkets for months, and then selling the food they had stolen to smaller shops.

"The game is now over for the food bank robbers. All twenty-three members of their shameless gang are being questioned by the police," finished Mum. "Food banks nationwide are safe again."

"Good!" I said, feeling my insides swell up with pride.

Putting the newspaper down, Mum reached out and hugged me and Ashley again.

"Oh! I am so proud of my two little heroes," Mum

whispered, before telling us to get ready quickly for school. But before I left the kitchen table, I stared at Mum's face for just as long as I could. I had nearly forgotten what it felt like to see Mum smiling her real smile. And I didn't ever want to forget it.

Then, at school, things got even better.

In assembly, the Breakfast Club and everyone else gave me and Harriet and Krish and even Ashley a huge round of applause, and Mrs. Bell called us up onto the stage to get some special certificates for bravery and determination!

And then something happened that was so amazing and so spectacular that I thought I had to be dreaming.

Because it wasn't Mrs. Bell who gave us our certificates. Instead, she told the school that a very special guest wanted to do that and pointed to the back of the hall.

Mr. Ramjit and Maureen the dinner lady gave everyone a wave and threw open the hall doors.

And there he was!

Noah Equiano—the REAL Noah Equiano!

The school burst into cheers as everyone got to their feet, and Krish screamed, "NO WAAAAAAAAAAAAAAAAAAAAAAY!"

The real Noah Equiano came jogging up to the stage, waving at everyone and making Harriet hiccup so badly she had to clamp her hands over her mouth to make it stop.

It turned out that Noah Equiano hadn't come to our school just to give me and Krish and Harriet and Ashley a certificate. He had come to tell us that he had been a member of the Breakfast Club and the Free School Meals Club too. And that because we had been so brave and had helped hundreds of food banks by stopping the thieves, he wanted to invite us to Parliament so we could help every child in the country get the food they needed to keep them strong and healthy and have an equal chance to do all the things they wanted to do—not just at school but after they finished school too.

And after Harriet stopped hiccupping, and Krish stopped screaming silently, and I could speak again, we all shouted, "YES!!"

Because who would say no to going on an adventure with the Equalizer to make sure that no one like me, or Ashley, or anyone at the Breakfast Club ever went to bed hungry again? Not anyone I can think of.

Except, maybe, a thief.

AUTHOR'S NOTES

THE DAY WE MET THE QUEEN

People often ask me if *The Day We Met the Queen* and its prequel, *The Boy at the Back of the Class,* were difficult to write. Because as you will have read, the children at the heart of this adventure are faced with trying to understand and even tackle one of the gravest, most worrying developments of our world: the harsh treatment of refugees.

The truth is, the ideas for both stories weren't difficult to forge at all. Not because writing comes easily to me. (It doesn't.) Or because this is a story I had planned and plotted to write for years. (I hadn't.) But because every single character you have met in this story is based on someone I have met in real life—barring the Queen, of course! (Though I *did* visit Buckingham Palace for a garden party and stood twenty feet away from her many, many years ago. But I'm not sure that counts as actually "meeting" her!)

Ahmet, who was inspired by a baby I met in the refugee camps of France in 2016; Michael, Tom, Josie, and the narrator, based on friends I had in school and have made in the camps; the angry protestors and horrid MP shouting mean things about refugees—none of them are figments of my imagination. They are all real to me, because the situation they are in and the people they represent are real.

We live on a planet where over 80 million people have been forced to leave their beautiful homes, and sometimes even their countries, to try to find somewhere safe to restart their lives. (Over 80 percent of refugees never cross the borders of their country. They look for a safe space in nearby towns or cities and are labeled "internally displaced" refugees.) Many must relocate because of climate change disasters like earthquakes, forest fires, and tsunamis; or because wars are tearing their lands apart and killing their loved ones; or because of political persecution by a government they don't agree with; or even because companies and other countries are taking away their land and wealth and food.

As if it weren't horrible enough for someone to suddenly find themselves in danger, without a home or the people they love most in the world, what hurts perhaps more deeply is how other people, countries, and politicians react. Despite international laws in place telling every government, every country, every leader, that it is a duty to help refugees—to welcome and take care of them—until they can return home again safely, too few countries abide by these laws. Instead, they break their own human rights rules, put up borders and walls, tell refugees they can't use their passports or money to get to somewhere safe legally, and treat them like criminals for daring to try to survive. They even relabel refugees as "migrants" (people who *choose* to move because they want to, not because they have to), as if refugees *choose* to live in horrible places for months, or risk their lives at sea, or be chased and put into jails or detention centers.

In my work with refugee aid teams across northern France, I have seen refugee children—from babies to toddlers to ten-year-olds like Ahmet—looking for food or somewhere warm to sleep. Many are without their parents, traveling with aunts and uncles or injured grandparents, and are forced to live in muddy, freezing fields or under trees and bushes. And while they are doing this, they are called names and treated cruelly by local police and governments, too. It is only thanks to some very brave heroes who are out in the "camps" every day, distributing tents and sleeping bags and hot food and friendship, that any of these children and the grown-ups around them are able to stay alive at all.

I know you will agree with me when I say that none of this should be happening. Everyone deserves a home that is safe, and all children deserve a chance do the things we in more fortunate countries might take for granted, like go to school, play with friends, read stories, eat sweets, have mini fights with their brothers and sisters, get told off by their parents and teachers—and yes, maybe even visit a queen. And they should be able to do all those things without being hated for who they are and the journeys they have been forced to make.

To be a refugee, like Ahmet, is to be someone searching

for family, for peace, for humanity and kindness—and above all, friendship. Because those things, which are so very important to all of us, have been taken away—stolen from them, in ways few of us can imagine.

I hope that in the process of reading this short story, lots of questions and thoughts have popped into your mind. Questions and thoughts that I trust you will be brave enough to explore and talk about at school and maybe even at home too.

Because the truth is, for every Ahmet out there being called names or being bullied, there are hearts just like the one the narrator of this story has—along with Michael, Josie and Tom—waiting to help and defend and stand up for them.

I get to work with hearts just like that every single day, so I can spot them quite easily. And I have a sneaky feeling that you possess just such a heart: one that the world and all its refugees are in need of. And one any Queen would be lucky to meet!

THE GREAT FOOD BANK HEIST

What Are Food Banks?

DID YOU KNOW? In the United States today, over 38 million people (nearly 12 percent of the entire country!) and 12 million children live in homes that are struggling with food poverty. Millions of people have to skip meals completely.

In "The Great Food Bank Heist," Nelson's mum works as a nurse, but at the end of some months she doesn't have enough money to buy all the things her family needs. So they have to visit a food bank for help.

Food banks provide emergency food relief. Feeding America, a food bank charity, has more than two hundred giant warehouses that store millions pounds worth of food, and 60,000 active food banks delivering food and meals across the country, from Puerto Rico to Washington. There are many more food banks run by other charities and local community centers. They are able to help because thousands of very kind people donate to food banks at places such as supermarkets, schools, places of worship, and doctors' offices every day. Lots of supermarkets and local shops and restaurants also donate millions of pounds of food every year.

That's why food banks are special—they are made

up entirely of gifts given by people wanting to help other people. If you would like to learn more about food banks and how they help children like Nelson, visit feedingamerica.org.

Why Do People Need to Use Food Banks?

That's a good question! The United States is a very wealthy country—one of the richest countries in the world, according to some measurements. It is a country where there is lots of food being produced and sold and distributed.

But it is also a country that wastes more food than any other country in the world! Nearly 40 *million* tons of food—that's about 40 percent of the entire US food chain—are thrown away every year.[1] So why do we still have millions of people struggling with food poverty?

The answer is that food poverty is not just how much food is available in a country. It is part of a much bigger problem. Millions of families across the United States are struggling to pay their rent or bills for water and fuel. They may be waiting for the government to act faster to help them; they may be unable to find a job, or like Nelson's mum, they may have a landlord who keeps increasing their rent and as a result find themselves in debt. Because of problems like these, there is often not enough money to cover every cost, even when all the grown-ups in a home are working.

---

1 *rts.com/resources/guides/food-waste-america

This is a situation that can happen to anyone. People who need to use food banks should never feel ashamed because they need help. It's actually one of the bravest things in the world to do: to ask for help when you need it.

What Are Breakfast Clubs?

As the name suggests, breakfast clubs are . . . clubs that serve breakfast! Yum! They often open an hour before school starts, and most are run in schools and overseen by lovely teachers, teaching assistants, catering staff, and volunteers. You may have heard that breakfast is the most important meal of the day! It is, after all, the meal that breaks your night's fast (hence the name) and gives your body the energy it needs to get going for the day ahead.

But for many of us, breakfast becomes a missed meal—usually because everyone is in a rush to get out of the door! For many parents and guardians who work, there simply isn't time to get breakfast ready for everyone. And for those who are struggling with food poverty, there may not be enough food in the house to provide a nutritious breakfast. In the United States, the School Breakfast Program (SBP) is a federally funded program that helps millions of children every year get a delicious breakfast every morning.

That's why breakfast clubs are one of the best kinds of clubs around. They help parents and guardians stop worrying, and they give everyone a chance to start the day with a full tummy.

Three Ways You Can Help Food Banks and Breakfast Clubs

DID YOU KNOW? While food banks may have "food" in the title, they don't give just things to eat and drink to the people they help. They also provide essential items like toiletries, hygiene products, diapers, and baby food. Feeding America and lots of other food banks also offer hot meals, deliver food boxes to people's homes, and give free lunches at school to children who may not be getting enough to eat at home.

Lots of breakfast clubs also provide space for children and young people to do their homework before school starts, as well as games and books.

Here are three ways you can help your local food banks and your school:

1. Find out what is needed.

To make sure people are getting what they need, it's better to ask and know for sure rather than to make a guess. This also stops the creation of extra food waste.

To find a local food bank, visit feedingamerica.org/find-your-local-foodbank and type in your zip code. This will tell you where you can donate and what they really need.

For your school breakfast club, ask your teacher or principal if there is anything that is needed (games, books, maybe even computers) that you can donate or help raise funds for.

2. Help tackle "holiday hunger."

During the school holidays, when there are no free school meals and fewer breakfast clubs available, many families find it even more difficult to access the food they need. Lots of businesses, charities, and faith groups work even harder at these times to raise donations and distribute help to local families.

If you or someone you know needs help accessing food during the holidays, No Kid Hungry USA has a brilliant map of where you can find free, healthy meals being served by organizations in your community. Visit nokidhungry.org/find-free-meals to find help or to learn how you can help them in their work.

3. Ask your family to join the Campaign to End Hunger at feedingamerica.org/take-action.

By making a pledge to help end hunger, you and your family can hear about both local and national campaigns to encourage the US government to help end food poverty and get information on other things you can do.

ACKNOWLEDGMENTS

No story—and especially not those that need to be adjusted, nurtured, and reforged overseas—is ever produced alone. Both of these stories were inspired by some of the wonderful children and volunteers I have the great honor to work with, be it in refugee camps, in women's refuges, or in food banks and schools. The fact that I get to write and publish them at all is thanks to a world of amazing hearts who are equally passionate about getting these stories out into the world.

With that in mind, my deepest thanks must go to Silvia Molteni, Lena McCauley, and Alisa Bathgate, my UK teams, for helping these stories come into existence at all; Beverly Horowitz at Penguin Random House for having such a deep faith in my stories as to bring these two shorter ones together (something I never envisioned!); Lydia Gregovic for bearing with my disappearances and appearances so beautifully and generously to ensure these two book babies came to be as they are; Rebecca Gudelis for being a part of my US adventures from the word go; Pippa Curnick for gifting such a gorgeously clever cover; and all my magical Delacorte Press family, who work so hard to let my book worlds go on spinning, night and day.

And no book containing the characters of either Ahmet or Nelson could ever go without containing a prayer of love and hope for Baby Raehan—the refugee baby of Northern France whose memory inspired the character of Ahmet in *The Day We Met the Queen*—and little Meghan, Melissa, and David, who inspired the characters of Nelson and his sister in *The Great Food Bank Heist.* Meeting them changed me in ways I will never fully be able to fathom. And in their memories, I hope these stories will go on inspiring questions, quests for answers, and maybe even solutions, so that no more children are ever called on to suffer the same hurts.

Here's hoping. . . .

ABOUT THE AUTHOR

ONJALI Q. RAÚF is the founder and CEO of Making HerStory, a UK nonprofit that works to fight human trafficking and gender-based abuses and crimes, and O's Refugee Aid Team, which supports frontline refugee aid response teams across Northern France, Greece, and beyond. She is the author of *The Boy at the Back of the Class, The Star Outside My Window, The Night Bus Hero,* and *Heroes Like Us.* She lives in the UK, and in 2022 was awarded an MBE by the Queen—which means that she may get to meet her for real, and maybe ask her some questions too, just like Ahmet and his friends!